Once and for Always

By

Linda Jones

ISBN: 978-1-916820-42-5

This is a work of fiction. Names and characters are the product of the author's imagination and any resemblance to actual persons, living or dead, is entirely coincidental.

The views expressed in this work are solely those of the author and do not necessarily reflect the views of the publisher, and the publisher hereby disclaims any responsibility for them.

www.publishnation.co.uk

Acknowledgements

My thanks as always to the many historians who have documented this period. Any inconsistencies are entirely my errors or tweaks to fit the narrative.

Also thanks to Janet, my proof reader, for her patience.

Other books by Linda Jones

The Angel
Authorhouse March 2007

ISBN:978-1-4259-9772-9

Witch Hunt

Xlibris 2011

ISBN:978-1-4628-9650-9

The Lost Heiress

Diadem Books 2015

ISBN:978-1-3264-5735-8

The Mysterious Miss Hawthorne

Diadem Books 2017

ISBN:978-1-3264-4939-1

Tenuous Connections

Diadem Books 2017

ISBN:978-0-244-95360-7

Heartsong

Diadem Books 2018

ISBN:978-0-244-71718-6

Children of Eden

Diadem Books 2019

ISBN:978-0-244-80410-7

Claiming Samantha

Diadem Books 2020

ISBN-13:9798581385104

Chapter 1

Cambridge. Spring 1863

Bea averted her eyes from the closed shutters and the black wreath custom demanded as a sign of mourning. Both would be taken down tomorrow. She needed no reminders that she had now lost both parents.

Tears blurred her vision as she unlocked the shop door. No cheerful tinkle welcomed her entrance, the muffled bell another nod to convention.

Her two companions followed her inside, a middle-aged woman and a gangling youth. The boy turned back to close and bolt the door.

'No. Leave the bolt, Freddie. There will be no customers today and Mr Fleming will be along after…' Bea could not bring herself to say, 'after the burial.' Females were not expected to be at an interment, even of a beloved father.

The older woman laid a comforting hand on Bea's shoulder. 'Bear up, love. I'll go and make some tea.'

Bea managed a watery smile. Tea! Dora's panacea for all ills, woes and problems. Tea and sympathy. Dora Cotton had been with the family for as long as Bea could remember. She was more than a servant but not quite one of the family. Dora gave Bea's shoulder a squeeze and nodded to Freddie to follow her through a curtained archway.

Bea made her way across the dim interior of the bookshop, removed her cloak and bonnet and laid them across the counter. She felt so tired although all she had done was to sit through a brief service.

It had been a quiet funeral. John Hastings had been a quiet man. Polite and helpful to his customers but basically very shy. His warm, loving personality only emerged in the privacy of his home and in the presence of family and close friends. The sudden death of Grace, his beloved wife, had crushed him. Only Bea's gentle encouragement, Dora's brisk cajoling and Freddie's cheerful expectation that life would go on as usual had dragged him from his bed each morning. He had drifted through the days, becoming more and more withdrawn until finally he just stopped living. He was forty-four. Much too young to die.

With a sigh Bea reached up to pull down the hanging lamp. The poor light did not bother her. She knew every inch of the bookshop. It had been her nursery, school room and place of work. But she had recently rearranged the furniture which could be a hazard to the unwary and Robert Fleming would be here soon.

It was sheer luck that Uncle Rob, as Bea thought of him, had arrived in time for the funeral. Guided by Dora, Bea had looked through her father's desk to find his old friend's address. Rob was a frequent but erratic visitor who travelled far and wide. There had been no guarantee the letter would reach him in time.

Bea had just lit the lamp when there was a sharp rap on the door. It opened and the draught made the lamp flame flicker. 'I did not expect you soon,' Bea said and carefully replaced the glass chimney before turning around.

The man moving towards her was not Rob.

'I am glad you were expecting me, Beatrice,' Mr Tanner smirked. He was the landlord's agent, a small officious man with sharp features and a twitchy nose that reminded Bea of a rodent. She called him the Weasel. His dark eyes made Bea squirm. They darted around inquisitively and usually came to rest on her bosom.

Bea ignored his familiarity. It would not do to antagonise him before the lease was transferred. As politely as she could, Bea said, 'We are closed today, Mr Tanner. I will need to see you about transferring the lease but it was my father's funeral today and I really need a little time alone.'

Tanner moved closer and Bea retreated behind the counter. 'That is what I have come about. I need to know when you will be ready to leave.'

'Leave?' Bea echoed. 'I will not be leaving. Once the lease is transferred into my name, I shall continue to run the shop.'

Tanner shook his head and sucked in a breath through his prominent front teeth. 'A woman can't run a business.'

'As you know I have been running the business for some time. What difference would it make?'

Tanner moved closer and rested his arms on the counter. Bea realised she had trapped herself. The wall was at her back. She would have to pass him to get to the door. If he reached out, he could touch her. *Don't panic,* she thought and picked up the heavy inkwell. She weighed it in her hand and looked pointedly at Tanner arms and he took a step back.

'It would still not be right. Your father is no longer here to protect you.' He shook his head and gave her a n assessing glance. 'A young woman living here alone. Think of your reputation.' His voice lowered to an oily croon. 'I could find you a nice little house. Somewhere quiet.' His eyes fastened on her bosom in silent confirmation of what he was suggesting.

'What of my reputation then? And I will not be living alone.'

Over Tanner's shoulder she could see Rob Fleming standing in the doorway. It gave her courage and Bea decided to make her position clear. 'Mr Tanner, I would like to take over the lease and I will appeal directly to my landlord if necessary. The bank will assure him the business is sound and the rent paid promptly as usual. I really do not see a problem.'

'Lord Ridgeworth leaves everything to me.' Tanner was becoming annoyed. 'You will soon see a problem when you find yourself out on the street.'

'Do you have a problem at this moment, Miss Hastings?' Fleming's voice held a note of concerned enquiry.

Tanner spun around ready to say the shop was closed but the sight of a large, prosperous looking man gave him pause. He knew Mr Fleming by sight and reputation. Robert Fleming presented an imposing figure. He was tall and broad shouldered. His face was in shadow but he radiated authority. Not a man to mess with.

'I am here on business,' Tanner muttered. He noticed the valise in Fleming's hand and sneered. 'Like that, it is? Not alone after all.' He turned to Bea, 'What of your reputation now?'

Fleming's bag hit the floor with a thud and he crossed the room with surprising speed. Tanner scooted to one side, colliding with a chair on his way to the door. Fleming blocked his path and loomed over the rent collector. 'I suggest you leave before you insult the lady any further.' Fleming moved aside and Tanner sidled past. Safely at the door Tanner had more to say. 'Lady! A shop girl who says one thing and acts like….' His finally words faded into the distance as he ran – Mr Fleming hot on his heels.

Bea sagged against the wall torn between hope that Uncle Rob caught the Weasel and fear of what would happen if he did. Tanner was already disinclined to grant her the lease and being assaulted was not likely to change his mind.

What would she do then? Would Lord Ridgeworth refuse to grant her the lease? She had never seen him. She remembered the property changing hands a few years ago but the new owner had never visited.

Bea knew that Uncle Rob would not allow her to become homeless but what would she do with all the books? Would any other landlord grant a lease to a woman?

Bea looked around at the filled shelves. The original stock had been her mother's dowry but it had changed over the years. Her father had had no head for business and left the management of the shop to his wife. He was only really at ease dealing with the scholarly gentlemen from the university. In a deep discussion of the Classics or his beloved Shakespeare, he lost all his shyness. A simple enquiry of a more personal nature threw him into confusion.

Grace Hastings was more self-assured and with a good head for business. She never dominated her more retiring husband and always asked his opinion before making any decisions but he usually told her to do what she thought best. With his vague agreement Grace had gradually introduced a wide range of modern fiction, travelogues and journals as well as easy reading for beginners.

The introduction of cheap postage gave many of the working class an incentive to learn to read. To encourage them, Grace had added new furniture and gave reading classes for a small fee. Bea hoped to continue and expand the enterprise.

Oh, Mama, Bea, thought. *He would not have dared to insult you.*

Grace Hastings was a lady born. Even a birth defect that had left her with an under-developed left side did not diminish either her dignity or her energy. Bea was sure her mother had loved her but she had never been demonstrative, even in private. She had taught Bea all she knew to prepare her for the future, whether that future was to run a bookshop or to eventually take her rightful place in society.

Bea's depressing thoughts were interrupted by the return of Mr Fleming. He closed and bolted the door. She went to greet him with outstretched hands.

'Don't look so worried,' he laughed. 'I did not give the little rat his just deserts. I have persuaded him to come back tomorrow.'

Bea laughed too. 'I call him the Weasel.' She sobered. 'But what good will it do? He will give me notice and all my plans will come to naught.'

Rob gave her a hug. 'The fact that you have plans is a positive. We just need to work out how to implement them.'

His confidence heartened Bea. She had known him all her life. He seemed an unlikely friend for her shy, retiring father but they shared a similar background. Both were from minor branches of aristocratic families that needed to make their own way in the world. Rob was a prosperous business man although Bea was not sure what he actually did. From the things she had heard him discuss with her parents it seemed very diverse – investing, buying and selling and generally knowing how to make money. Bea assumed he had a home somewhere but always seemed to be returning from or setting out on another journey.

Dora came bustling through the archway. 'It's all ready for when Mr … Oh, you are here already, sir,' she added when she noticed Rob. 'You go straight up to the parlour. Freddie will take your bag up later.'

'I won't be staying, Dora.' He winked at Bea, 'We would not want to give anyone the wrong impression.'

'Pooh!' Dora snorted. 'You are almost family. Everyone knows you stay here.'

'Things have changed but I have matters to sort out with Bea and will return tomorrow.'

'You will have your supper first!' Dora declared with the familiarity of long acquaintance. 'Now, get up those stairs before the tea over-brews.'

They followed Dora through the arch into a square hallway lit by a window that had replaced the original front door when the property was converted into a shop. A wide staircase led to the upper floors and beyond the stairs a corridor led to the kitchen and the old butler's pantry where Freddie slept.

It was a substantial house. The parlour was large and furnished with comfortable, good quality furniture. Freddie stood up from where he had been tending the fire. He was a pleasant-faced lad of fourteen. He grinned at Fleming and said hello before leaving the room.

'He improves every time I see him,' Rob remarked, taking a seat at the small table laid with supper. As they ate, they talked about Freddie who had joined the household much in the way a stray cat accepts a plate of scraps and never leaves. He had, mostly, lost his bad manners and worse language and rewarded the family for taking him off the streets by loyal service and devotion to Bea.

Dora was a similar case. She had come to clean and earn money that her husband spent on drink and gambling. After he was killed in a drunken brawl Dora became cook, housekeeper and general assistant, turning her hand to any task Mrs Hastings found difficult. And loving Bea.

Bea wanted to discuss her predicament but Rob kept the conversation to neutral topics, urging Bea to eat her supper. Only after the meal was finished did he bring up the subject of the plans she had mentioned.

'Well,' she began. 'Mama had already started to expand the range of books. I doubt Papa even noticed that we now sell novels and periodicals.' Bea smiled, 'You know what he was like with people who just wanted to browse and gossip.'

Rob chuckled. 'I suppose that explains all the extra furniture downstairs.'

'Yes, we have a reading group with people who want to learn to read. If I could go ahead, I would close the learned section altogether and start a lending library. We have contacts who would supply us with second-hand books at a low price. Hopefully, that would lead to people wanting to buy their own new copies.'

'What do you see as your main problem'

'The Weasel. And the lease.'

As she stacked the used crockery Bea asked, 'What am I going to do Uncle Rob? This my home. I love the books and encouraging people to enjoy them too.'

He guided her to a seat by the fire and stood and looked at her for a minute. Black clothing did her no favours. Her naturally fair complexion looked pasty with dark smudges under her eyes. Eyes that usually sparkled with intelligence but were now dimmed by grief and worry. She was neither plain nor outstandingly pretty. Her facial features resembled her mother with a straight little nose and a firm chin.

On the plus side, she was graceful and had an unconscious charm. He had seen her grow from an inquisitive child into a well-read and capable woman. Her intelligence came from both parents, nurtured by their careful teaching.

On the downside, her upbringing had been that of a lady combined with the practicalities of a working woman. The shop would make her an embarrassment to her aristocratic relations – if they could find any willing to accept her. The same applied if turned on its head – it would inhibit any advances from lower class men. Unless, like Tanner, they saw her as an easy mark. Unfortunately, certain upper-class men were also likely to think her unworthy of respect.

'Leave it until tomorrow,' Rob advised. 'There is always a solution if you think clearly.'

That was so like his normal manner. He gathered facts, assessed the pros and cons and acted decisively.

Bea escorted him to the street door, said goodnight and watched him walk away. She closed and locked the door, dowsed the lamp and went up to bed, confident that by morning her Uncle Rob would have solved the problem.

Chapter 2

Rob arrived at 8.30am next morning, just as Freddie was removing the shutters. He told Freddie to leave the closed sign on the door and only admit Mr Tanner until they had finished discussing some business.

'You have thought of something!' Bea cried happily from her place behind the counter. 'What is it?'

'Not so fast. I have to ask you a few questions.' He glanced at Freddie lurking by the door. 'Upstairs I think.'

They sat in opposite chairs by the parlour fire. It was so familiar Bea expected her Papa to join them at any minute. Rob steepled his fingers and tapped them against his lips, a habit he had when thinking. For a moment Bea thought he had failed to find a solution and was wondering how to break the news. Before she could panic, he lowered his hands and spoke.

'I know of several widows who run businesses in their own name.'

'I am not a widow. I am not even married.'

'Is there anyone you are interested in?'

Bea had a sudden vision of a golden-haired Adonis with twinkling blue eyes. She hastily tucked it back into the depths of her heart where it belonged. There was no point in hankering for the unattainable. 'No.'

Rob had been watching her face. 'Then I think you should marry me.'

Bea looked at him with a startled expression, eyes wide and mouth half open.

Rob laughed. 'It is not such a bad idea. It would not be a conventional marriage, more a partnership with the added protection of a husband in the background.' Bea was lost for words. 'It could work,' Rob assured her. 'We like each other. We could work well together.'

'I don't know what to say.'

''Yes, would be preferable. No, will take a little more thought.'

'Why would you do this for me?'

Rob looked at her kindly. 'Let us just say that I owe your father a debt I have never been able to repay. I will take care of you for his sake. I do not mean that to sound insulting or make you feel like a burden.'

Bea stared back at him, still in a state of shock. He was the same age asf her father although he looked much younger. He talked about his travels and the people he met but she knew next to nothing about his private life. She was glad he had not mentioned love. He was proposing a business arrangement, something she was familiar with. He had helped her Mama with her investments. Bea blinked rapidly. Was that what he wanted?

Rob laughed. 'I can see what you are thinking. I am not after your money, I have enough of my own. Nor do I want to interfere with your running of the shop. Everything you have will remain in your name.' He leant forward and took hold of her hand. 'Bea, I am really a very selfish person. Taking care of you will relieve my mind. My life will not change. I will come and go as I have done for years. I will give you any help you need but you will have to ask for it. Do you have an answer for me?'

Bea nodded. 'Yes. Mama and Papa trusted you. Thank you.'

'Good.' That was all. A deal done.

'Now,' Rob said getting to his feet. 'Shall we go and sort out your Weasel?'

'Not mine!' Bea declared with a shudder. 'Do you think he will give me the lease and leave me alone?'

Rob just looked at her with raised eyebrows. 'Have I not just said how things will go on?'

They were halfway down the stairs when they heard the shop bell tinkle. Tanner's insolent voice followed. 'You can keep your opinions to yourself, boy! Tell her to get down here. I have not got all day to waste.'

Freddie met them at the foot of the stairs. 'Bea.?' He looked worried.

'I know,' Bea said with a wry twist of her lips. 'We heard his greeting.'

'We won't be long,' Rob added. 'You can leave us know. Bea will tell you about it later.'

Tanner had made himself at home, relaxed on a chair with one ankle crossed over the opposite knee and a smirk on his face. It vanished as soon as Rob entered the shop behind Bea. Tanner shot to his feet. 'You again? Or have you been here all night?' Rob took a step forward but Tanner was closer to the door and refused to be intimidated. 'I have business to discuss with Miss Hastings.'

'Any business will be discussed with me.' Rob leaned back against the counter and continued. 'I believe your supposed problem with the lease if because Miss Hastings is a single lady.'

'I would not grant the lease to any woman,' Tanner declared, ignoring the distinction in terms. 'Business is for men.'

'I agree up to a point.' Rob remarked, casually examining his finger nails. 'The law is very dismissive of females. It does not take into account their ability and experience.' His stern gaze fastened on Tanner's face as he declared, 'Miss Hastings has both. You would not hesitate to grant the lease if she were a man. Or to her husband.' It was not a question.

'But she,' Tanner sneered with a jerk of his head towards Bea, 'ain't married.'

Rob stood away from the counter. 'She, if you are referring to Miss Hastings, will be my wife in the very near future.' Rob removed a card from his waistcoat pocket and offered it to Tanner.

The agent made no move to take it. 'And who might you be?' It was a silly question as everyone hereabout knew Mr Fleming was a friend of the family and frequent visitor.

'I might,' Rob replied slowly, 'be having a word with Lord Ridgeworth about your insulting behaviour to my future wife.' He stepped forward and waggled the card under Tanner's nose. 'There are my details. Please deal with the formalities without delay.'

Mr Fleming knowing Lord Ridgeworth took the wind out of Tanner's sails. He was down but not yet out. 'Is this true? Are your really going to marry her, er, Miss Hastings?' he added.

'Yes.'

Tanner knew when he was beaten. He took the card in his left hand but did not bother to glance at the name. He held out his right hand. 'Then I am happy to do business with you, Mr Fleming.'

Rob looked at the proffered hand with disgust. 'I do not shake hands until a deal is finalised.'

'Yes. Quite so.' Tanner shuffled towards the door. 'I'll see to this straight away.'

Bea waited until the door closed before letting out a long breath. 'Thank you. I thought he was going to insist on being a witness at the wedding.'

'Speaking of witnesses, may I suggest Mrs Cotton and Freddie. Does Freddie have another name?'

'He's not sure but his mother went by the name of Mrs Smith. Is he old enough?'

'Very original,' Rob said wryly. 'I don't see why he cannot be a witness. He can read and write his name, thanks to you and Grace.'

'When will we be married?' Bea asked, not quite looking at his face. She did not want to sound too eager but speed did appear necessary. 'And, please, I don't want a big fuss.'

'Neither do I and as soon as I can arrange it. Right answers wrong order,' Rob said with a smile. 'I shall need your birth certificate. Do you know where it is.'

Bea led the way back upstairs and to the room her father had used as a study. A strong box stood in one corner. 'I don't know where the key is.'

'Probably in John's desk,' Rob suggested.

It was the second time Bea had searched the desk but it still did not feel right.

'Bea,' Rob said gently, 'this is all yours now. You will have to go through it at some point. There may be correspondence. People who ought to be told of John's death.' He doubted anyone would be interested but he could not tell Bea that.

Bea found the key and handed it to Rob. She might have to go through the strong box as well but not yet.

The certificate was in an envelope along with her parent's marriage certificate and he mother's wedding ring. Bea felt tears welling up and brushed them away. 'Would you mind if we used Mama's ring? As ours is not to be a ………'

'I know what you mean, my dear. Buying you a ring would make it too personal. By all means wear your mother's ring if it makes you more comfortable. Shall I take the share certificates as well? It will probably take a week or so to get the details changed. You will have them back as soon as possible'.

Rob gathered up the documents and put them in his briefcase. Bea tucked the ring into her pocket. Keeping it close made the bizarre situation seem more real. All that was left in the box was her parents' marriage certificate and the small velvet roll that held her Mama's few pieces of jewellery. Bea would not be able to wear them yet as she would still be in mourning, even after the wedding. The strong box looked very empty. Was that the sum total of her parents' lives? How sad.

Rob looked at her with sympathy. The past few months had been traumatic for her but he would do all he could to give her security. 'It does no good to dwell on the past, Bea. Cheer up. Let's go and tell our witnesses.'

Freddie was over the moon at being asked to witness Bea's wedding. 'Can I get a new suit? And a hat?'

'Not a top hat,' Rob told the boy firmly. 'It would be a waste of money as you are unlikely to need it again.'

There was a loud knocking on the front door which still showed the closed sign.

'I'll go down with Freddie,' Rob said. 'That may be Tanner. If not, I'll wait.' He looked at Dora who had not said a word. 'You will want to tell Dora all about it.'

The two women were silent for a moment after the kitchen door closed. Dora looked as though she had received news of another death and Bea frowned. 'Aren't you going to congratulate me?'

'Not until I know what he meant by 'all about it'.'

It took a while. Dora listened until Bea ran out of words. 'Well? Bea prompted.

'I need a cup of tea and, if I may say so, you need to think carefully before you rush into this marriage.'

'I don't have time! Tanner will turn us out. What would we all do then?'

Dora kept her back turned as she busied herself with the tea things. 'You don't need to worry about me and Freddie.' She spun around. 'We would not leave you and together we can manage, somehow.' Dora sat down suddenly. 'Oh, Bea, have you asked yourself what Mr Fleming gets out of this?'

Bea laughed in relief. 'He said he owed a debt to Papa. Keeping me safe is his way of repaying that debt.'

'I still don't like it. What do you really know about him? You say he is going to change the deeds into your name. What if he changes them into his and disappears? What if Fleming is not his real name? Then where will you be?'

'Don't be silly. Papa has known him since boyhood. Mama would not have trusted him if there was anything shady in his past.' Bea frowned. 'Come to that I don't know very much about Papa's background. I know he has no family but you know how he always changed the subject if I asked about his early years.'

There was not much Dora did not know about the Hastings. She probably knew more about them than Bea herself. She had been Grace's confidant. In the days before she died Grace had opened her heart to the woman who had become her friend. 'Tell Bea as much as she needs to know. I have tried not to poison her mind about John's family. With luck she will never find out how he was treated.' Dora had given her word that she would always take care of Bea.

The rattle of the kettle lid jerked Dora back into action. She got up and made the tea and had just brought the pot to the table when Rob returned to the room.

He waved a folded paper. 'I'll be on my way now. You won't have any more trouble from Tanner. I have made it clear that although I may not be here all the time I will know if he does anything to upset you.'

He refused a cup of tea, kissed Bea's cheek and looked at Dora's serious face. 'This is the best I can do for Bea, Mrs Cotton. I know you care for her but in this you have to trust me to know what I am doing.' With a nod and a last smile at Bea he left again.

Chapter 3

That same afternoon Bea took the black wreath to lay on her parents' grave. The newly turned earth only bore a simple wooden marker. She would have to get the stonemason to amend the headstone which had only been set in place a few weeks ago.

Bea knelt down and started to talk. She knew her mother would approve of the marriage. Above all else Grace Hastings had been practical.

Bea had always been closer to her father. She could tell him things her Mama would scoff at.

'Am I doing the right thing?' Bea asked when she came to the end of her recital. They could not answer of course but she could not sense any disapproval. They had both known and trusted Rob. She had no option but to do the same.

Footsteps on the gravel path made Bea turn around. It was the vicar, Rev Robins. He waited at a distance until Bea started to rise and then moved forward to help her to her feet.

'I have just been to call on you,' he said. 'I was concerned as to what you had planned for the future. Now I hear you are to be married.'

'Yes. Mr Fleming is a friend of the family. I will be able to stay here and still run the bookshop.'

'Then I wish you well and look forward to meeting Mr Fleming soon.'

The Vicar accompanied her to the gate where they turned in different directions.

Bea did not have far to go. St Anne's Row was a wide lane that ran between the church yard and the grounds of Peakes University. The shops were on the university side. The houses opposite were smaller and leased out to private individuals.

Bea met several people on the short walk home. Freddie had been joyfully spreading the news with more emphasis on his new suit than the actual wedding. Polite congratulations, heavily tinged with curiosity, delayed her. Although the Hastings had lived quietly, they had not been reclusive. Bea and her Mama had attended church regularly and were members of the Parish

Charity group. They shopped and attended a few minor functions. Mr Hastings was less out-going. Most of his outdoor activities had been confined to solitary walks and visits to book sales. People were friendly but the family's obvious gentility created a barrier that few were willing to breach.

One exception was the daughter of the ironmonger. She was about twelve years' old and had not learned when it was impertinent to voice an opinion.

'I wouldn't want to marry an old man,' she told Bea. Then gave a knowing grin. 'But Mr Fleming is a fine figure. You won't find being his wife a burden.'

The implication was clear, making Bea blush. The girl giggled and ran back into her father's shop.

Bea hurried away. She was still rather flushed when she reached the bookshop and slipped upstairs before Dora could ask what was wrong.

Alone in her room Bea dabbed her face with cold water. She would have to get used to people thinking the marriage was consummated. She was not ignorant of what went on between a man and a woman. Her mother had explained the monthly bleeding and the reason for it. Bea's more explicit knowledge came from some of the books her father kept on a high shelf. They were shown to interested buyers in the privacy of the back room and Bea had grown curious and looked at them when no-one else was about.

Bea's blush returned in force. She could not imagine doing those things with Uncle Rob!

Her thoughts veered to another man. The golden-haired customer who had but had never forgotten him.

After that one meeting she had asked if it was possible to fall in love at first sight. They had been sitting around the dinner table at the time, the Hastings and Dora. Her mother had said it was better to get to know the man before making a commitment. Respect and affection would grow and endure.

Her father had said, 'Yes. If you are lucky you meet someone and know you will love once and for always.' Her parents had exchanged a look and Grace had hurried from the room. 'You will find that man, Bea,' her father said quietly. 'when you are older.'

Dora had waited until they were alone before giving her opinion. 'Don't you go falling for a pretty face and lovey words. That kind of love will blow up in your face and scar you for life.

Bea knew Dora spoke from experience.

With hindsight Bea wondered if her parents had done the same. They were not demonstrative but Bea was sure they had loved each other. Her father had lost the will to live after his beloved wife died.

Bea's heart was the kind that wanted once and always. Which did not bode well for the future. The customer, Mr Simon Armitage, was older and had only spoken a few words to her. To her knowledge, Mr Armitage had never visited the shop again. But that first rush of feeling had never dimmed. She had seen him briefly a few years later and although he had not recognised her, he was still firmly settled in her heart.

Bea was glad Uncle Rob, Bea laughed quietly, she really would have to stop thinking of him as an uncle. She was glad Rob had not mentioned love. He was fond of her. That would have to be enough.

Rob did not return the next day or the one after. Doubts took hold of Bea's mind. Not helped by Dora's silent sympathy. *What had she done?* She had given all her worldly assets to a man she really did not know. His name was on the lease. Dora's remark about it being his real name began to make awful sense. Rob did not want anything to do with the shop. If he was not really Mr Fleming, who was he and how could she find him and reclaim her possessions?

Bea tried to reassure herself with the fact that her parents had known him for years. But that only raised other questions. Were they who they said they were? There were no birth certificates. Bea was not sure when compulsory registration had become law but had a feeling it was quite recent. Had her life been a complete hoax?

In an effort to calm her fears, Bea went back to the strongbox to look at her parent's marriage certificate. The document confirmed that Grace Alice Conlyn, had married John Arthur Hastings at St Adolph's Church in Killdonny, Ireland, in 1842. That accorded with what her mother had told her about her own youth. Grace's father had been Baron Conlyn so her name had to be right. And her father was recorded as living at the same address.

That did not seem to make sense.

Bea thought back to what she knew of her mother's background. Grace's handicap had been an embarrassment to her widowed father and he had spent very little time at home. He refused to let Grace go into London society where he spent most of his time. Grace had never sounded unhappy or resentful when she spoke of her girlhood but it must have been lonely. Of her meeting with John Hastings Grace had only said he was her father's secretary and that they had married after her father died of a sudden heart attack. Given the fact that his employer rarely went home, Grace and John could not have known each other very well.

It did surprise Bea to learn that Grace was seven year's older than her husband. If she had ever thought about it, Bea would have guessed her father to be the elder. He had not looked particularly old. His hair was still thick with only a sprinkling of grey at the temples, it was just that he was so set in his ways and immersed in the study of ancient literature. Her mother on the other hands had been interested in the people she met and was open to new ideas. With such diverse natures, Bea had often wondered what they saw in each other.

That still left a big question mark against where her father originally came from, why he was still living at Conlyn after the Baron died and how he came to be such a close friend of Robert Fleming who came from Scotland.

It was all very unsettling. Bea slept badly and could not concentrate. The shop remained closed with an added note saying, 'until further notice.' Would it ever reopen?

Before she could go completely out of her mind Rob walked calmly into the shop late on the third day. Overcome with relief Bea threw herself into his arms.

'What's wrong?' he asked. 'Has Tanner been bothering you again?'

Bea stood back. 'I was beginning to think you were not coming back.'

'Bea,' he said reproachfully. 'I said there were things to arrange. They take time. I am sorry you have been worried. Set your mind at ease. We will be married tomorrow.'

Bea felt guilty for doubting him and almost lost track of what he was saying. He had said he would take care of everything. And he had. The wedding was to be a civil ceremony. 'I thought you would prefer that to making vows in church.' He told her the time of the ceremony and asked what she planned to wear.

Bea had been so consumed by the doubt that there would actually be a wedding, she had not given clothes a thought.

'I am still in mourning. I will wear my best black gown.'

'As you wish.' Black did not flatter Bea but if it made her more comfortable, he would not protest. He gave Bea a hug. 'Until tomorrow, dear girl.' Then he was gone again.

Bea's wedding was like nothing she had ever imaged. Not that she had ever attended a wedding but only a fool could be unaware that it involved a lot of planning. Bea had a niggling feeling that she would have liked to have been consulted and then rebuked herself for being petty. Rob's arrangements were exactly what she would have chosen. She just was not used to having decisions made for her.

Bea's wedding day began with grey sky and the threat of rain. Somewhere she had heard the phrase, Happy is the bridge the sun shines on. As this was not a real wedding, just the sealing of a contract between two people who liked and respected each other perhaps she did not need to rely on the weather to ensure a happy future.

Rob arrived in good time and they walked to the Town Hall, followed by Dora and Freddie. They were shown into a plainly furnished but highly polished room. The official in charge could be described in the same way. He was very thin with a shiny bald head and wearing a suit that was rubbed at the cuffs. He asked them to sit down while he checked a few details and then asked Bea and Rob to stand before his desk. The ceremony, if that was not too grand a word, was brief and conducted in a business-like manner. The registrar kept his eyes on a spot somewhere above and behind them and recited the words in a bored tone. Dora and Freddie were told to sign the register. The only moment he showed interest was when Freddie took the pen from Dora's hand and dipped it in the inkwell. 'Make your mark there,' the official said, placing a finger on the exact spot.

'I can write and read!' the lad said indigently. Even so the official checked the signatures before handing Rob the certificate and received an envelope in return. He did not offer to shake hands or congratulate them.

Freddie barely waited for them to exit the building before giving vent to his feelings. 'What a cheek. Just because we are not posh there was no need for him to talk down to me.' Bea understood his annoyance. Freddie had worked very hard to overcome his early lifestyle. To him, being able to read and write made him almost a gentleman, not someone to be looked down upon.

Bea reassured him he looked very smart in his ready-made suit. It was a bit on the large side to allow for growth but Freddie was very proud of it.

Dora was more subdued. 'I would hardly call that a wedding. Are you sure it is legal?' she asked Rob. He waved the folded certificate, 'This is all the proof we need.' He placed Bea's hand in the crook of his arm and smiled. 'Mrs Fleming will you join me for a celebration?'

Dora laughed and Bea turned her head, just in time to see Dora give a little curtsey and accept Freddie's proffered arm.

Rob took them to a nearly hotel for a special lunch then they went back to the shop. Bea and Rob went up to the parlour as he said they had things to discuss.

Without wasting time, Rob gave Bea the certificate. 'Keep that somewhere safe. The share certificates will take a week or so and will be returned in your name.' Rob looked at her seriously. 'Do you know what they are worth?' When Bea replied, 'Not exactly,' he mentioned a sum that made her eyes pop.

'And it is all mine? It's a fortune.'

'Not really but it is enough for you to live comfortably if you ever wish to close the shop.'

'Thank you. That is hardly enough for what you are doing for me. But thank you is all I can think of.'

Rob shrugged it aside and they discussed other details. The shop sign was to be amended to read, *R.R & B.G. Fleming.* He gave her the address of a dealer who would take all the academic books and suggested Bea might like to have a small stationery section. 'If people are going to read and write they might as well purchase their stationery from you. There were a few more odds and ends to clear up before Rob asked, 'Have you been through your father's desk? Was there any correspondence or business that needs to be dealt with?

Bea shook her head. 'I cannot bring myself to do it yet. But I will.' Bea frowned. 'You sound as though you expect there to be something important.'

'John was very … Well, let us say he kept things close to his chest. If there is anything to worry about you have my card. I will come by from time to time as usual. Often enough to keep Tanner in check and avoid curiosity. Your neighbours are used to my visits and any censure will fall on my head for neglecting you.'

It was the perfect opportunity for Bea to ask what Rob knew of her father's early life but Rob had gone on to tell her about a trip he was planning and the chance was lost.

It was comfortingly familiar and the conversation drifted on to other, everyday topics until the light began to fade and Dora came up to say she had laid their supper in the dining room. 'There is no need for formally, Dora. It would not be the first time I have eaten in the kitchen,' Rob said.

She wagged a finger at him, 'You know Mr and Mrs Hastings always dressed in the evening and took their meal in the dining room' She laughed, 'And it will not be the first time you have done so. So, I'll have no more of your nonsense. Bea, it is time you got out of that dreary black and put on something pretty.'

Pretending to be chastened, the newly married pair did as they were told, laughing all the way to their separate rooms.

Supper was relaxed, largely due to Rob's sensitivity. He had known Bea for all her life and could read her thoughts. She was worrying about bedtime and if he was going to claim a husband's rights. He did not put it into words but managed to calm her fears by casually referring to your room and my room.

Later, alone in her bed, Bea pondered on the events of the day. She did not feel married. To all intents and purposed Rob was still Uncle although he had laughed when it slipped out in conversation. She thought of all the things she could do without having to ask permission. If things went wrong, she would only have herself to blame. Rob would always be in the background ready to save her.

Chapter 4

Cambridge, March 1866

Bea stood behind the counter experiencing an awful sense of deja vu. The Weasel stood on the other side of the counter demanding to know when she would quit the premises. Since her marriage he had been studiously polite on the rare occasions they met. Now her was sneering, almost gloating as he waited for her answer.

It had come as a shock a couple of weeks ago when she received a letter, address to Mr Fleming, Lease Holder, saying that the lease was being cancelled. Compensation would be paid but the premises must be vacated by 31st March 1866. She had sent Rob a letter but had not yet received a reply.

'I am waiting for my husband.'

'Wait on,' Tanner replied. 'I reckon he has done a runner.'

'What do you mean?

'He hasn't been near since Christmas.'

Bea was annoyed that the agent had been monitoring Rob's visits and replied sharply. 'My husband travels widely but he is aware of the problem and will be here soon.'

'Nah! I reckon he is fed up with you. He never did stay above a day or two. Perhaps I was not missing much when you turned down my last offer.'

'How dare you!' Bea's voice had risen and Freddie came to the door of the back room. He was now seventeen and well built. He started towards Tanner but Bea placed a hand on his arm. It was like restraining a dog who had spied a rabbit. To calm Freddie, she kept her own temper in check and managed to say, with some semblance of politeness, 'Mr Tanner, please leave. There are still several weeks until the end of the month.'

'You heard Mrs Fleming,' Freddie growled. 'Leave now or I will help you to the door.'

Tanner retreated but when he was safely at the door he turned back. 'I've waited a long time for this, Miss High-and-mighty. Don't rush with the packing. I can get the bailiffs to do it for you.'

'What did he mean? Freddie asked. 'Why do you need to pack?'

'I will tell you later. When Dora gets back from shopping. Go back to what you were doing, please.'

Bea gave Freddie a gentle nudge and sat down to think.

She had seldom needed to write to Rob. Whenever she did, she marked the letter 'personal' as he had directed. It had always been acknowledged by a letter or by a visit.

More worrying was the length of his absence. Bea was so used to his erratic visits she had not kept a record of the dates. Christmas had indeed been the last one. And two weeks since she sent the letter. What could be keeping him? Perhaps he was ill or even abroad. Bea rejected the last. Rob always told her when he was leaving the country. She would give him one more day and then send a telegram.

Everything had gone so well over the last three years. Her lending library and reading classes kept her busy. Freddie had progressed so well he could be left in charge if she wanted to go out for the day. They were happy. Rob's visits were enjoyable but Bea had grown in confidence and did not need to lean on him.

You do now, a sneaky voice in her head insisted. *Suppose he does not get here by the end of the month? Tanner would relish seeing the bailiffs tossing your things onto the pavement.*

'I am not helpless!' She spoke aloud and thought for a moment Freddie might come back. When he did not, Bea ran though her options. There weren't many.

Unlike the time after her father's death, Bea was now a capable and respected businesswoman. Other book sellers dealt with her fairly. The dealer Rob had suggested had purchased all the learned books for a sum Bea had thought exorbitant. At the time she had been ignorant that some of the volumes in her father's private collection were quite valuable and she could have been cheated.

Rob had returned her share certificates and given advice when she wanted to invest her excess profits. She had security. They would never be destitute but time was running out.

How was she to find other premises within a few days? Even with Rob's support it would be difficult.

What if he is not coming back? Doubt whispered in her ear.

Of course, he was. He just had not yet received her letter. But Tanner had, inadvertently, given her a good piece of advice. She needed to start packing. If necessary, the books, stationery, even the furniture could go into storage whilst she found somewhere else.

Bea pulled herself together as the shop bell heralded the arrival of a customer. Putting on a professional smile, Bea rose and turned to see who it was.

The two fashionably dressed, elderly ladies were none of her regular customers. The larger of the two was dressed in black with a heavy veil covering her face. The other looked frail and carried a walking stick. 'How may I help you? Please take a seat.'

Black dress threw back her veil to reveal a face suffused with anger. 'You can explain why you are writing personal letters to my husband. My **deceased** husband!

'I don't understand. The only letter I have....' Bea stopped abruptly. Something was very wrong here.

The frail lady spoke. 'This is Mrs Robinson-Fleming. Your letter was forwarded to her while she was staying with me in Bath.'

Ignoring politeness Bea flopped into a chair, shaking her head as though that would remove the fog that threatened to envelop her. 'I don't understand. The name is wrong. The letter must have been misdirected.'

'What you need to understand, you hussy, is that you are posing as my husband's wife. You even have the gall to link your names above the door!'

The smaller lady guided her friend to a chair. 'Stay calm, Harriet.' To Bea she said, 'I am Lady Leith, a close friend.' Without asking permission she went and turned the door notice to 'closed'. 'You will not want anyone disturbing us while we sort out this mess.'

'You ae in enough trouble already,' Mrs Robinson-Fleming snorted. 'Mis-directed is no excuse. It was sent to his office and marked personal. It was not meant to reach me, was it?'

Bea's good manners finally brought her to her feet so she could curtsey.

'Oh, sit down,' Lady Leith said. 'You look ready to faint.' Lady Leith pulled another chair close to her friend and sat down. 'Now we will get to the bottom of this fiasco.'

'There must be some mistake,' Bea began and was cut short by the widow.

'Yes, yours!'

Lady Leith laid a hand on the widow's arm. 'We will not get anywhere if you keep making accusations. It is clear Miss Er… Oh, we will get back to that in a moment. It is clear you did not know Robert was already married.'

There was a degree of sympathy in Lady Leith's voice which Bea welcomed. This lady would at least listen.

'I married Rob three….'

'Stop referring to my husband in that familiar manner!'

Freddie appeared again. 'More trouble Bea?'

'No,' she said quickly. 'These ladies and I have something to discuss.' Bea glanced at her sympathiser. 'Would you come upstairs?'

'A good idea,' Lady Leith agreed.

Bea told Freddie to ask Dora to send up tea and then mind the shop. Then she led the way up to the parlour.

Mrs Robinson-Fleming was overweight and the climb left her with no breath for interruptions. Bea saw them settled and took a chair opposite. Taking advantage of the widow's wheezes, Bea began to explain.

'I married Mr Fleming three years ago. After my father died. They were old friends. He had visited us frequently over the years. I called him Uncle Rob. He offered marriage as a way for me to stay here. There was never any, er, intimacy between us.'

Mrs Robinson-Fleming had regained enough breath to say, 'Thank God for that.'

'Indeed. So, we do not have to worry about embarrassing additions?'

'Bastards.' The widow was gaining strength.

Bea had never heard the word spoken, knowingly, in her presence and certainly not by a lady. The coarseness stiffened Bea's spirit.

'No,' she said firmly. 'We had a business arrangement so I could continue to run the bookshop.'

'If it was a partnership why did you pretend to be married?'

'I didn't pretend. We were married in the Town Hall. I have a certificate to prove it. Shall I fetch it?'

Lady Leith shook her head. 'I don't see how that was obtained legally. Robert was married to his wife for over twenty years.'

'Of course, it was not legal, just another of Robert's schemes. I wonder how many more 'wives' are going to turn up on my doorstep.'

A tap on the door stopped her from continuing. Dora came in the tea tray and looked enquiringly at Bea. 'Thank you, Dora. I will pour.' The formality on top of Freddie's remarks made Dora reluctant to leave. Bea nodded and gave a tiny smile of reassurance. Dora left, closing the door with more than usual force.

A cup of tea and a chance to take in her surroundings had a calming effect on the widow. The furniture was good quality and well kept. There were paintings on the tastefully papered walls and flowers on a table by the window.

'Miss! What is your name?'

'I thought it was Mrs Fleming. I thought Robinson was a given name. I suppose I am still Miss Hastings.'

Dora returned. 'Excuse me but Mrs Adams is at the back door for her lesson. She says the closed sign is up.'

'Please give her my apologies. Say I have some unexpected visitors.'

Dora frowned and left reluctantly.

'Who was that,' Mrs Robinson-Fleming demanded. 'Can she be trusted not to talk?

'Dora, Mrs Cotton, is my greatest and most loyal friend. She was a witness at my wedding.'

Mrs Robinson-Fleming threw up her hands. 'Who else knows?'

'Well,' Bea replied with a shrug. 'Most of the people hereabouts, my customers and Freddie, my general helper. He was also a witness. And the land agent, of course. He transferred the lease into Rob's name.' Bea ignored the widow's snort at her use of Rob's name. But what else could she call him? He was not even Mr Fleming. Bea swallowed the tears that threatened. Rob was dead and the fact had only just hit her.

'When did he die?' Bea asked quietly.

'Two months ago. Not that is any of your business.'

Bea decided she did not like this woman and turned to the more sympathetic Lady.

'I think it is very much my business. I have been innocently involved in a bigamous ...' She could not complete the sentence. 'Oh, what am I to do? Will I be charged? I really did not know he was married.'

Bea's sincerity finally got through to Mrs Robinson-Fleming and she softened slightly. 'According to your letter, there is not much you can do. The business will close and you will have to move away. You will wish to avoid a scandal as much as I do.' She paused for a moment and stared at Bea for longer than was polite.

Bea tilted her head in enquiry and wondered what insult would come next.

It was not an insult exactly. The widow said, almost as though she was talking to herself. 'I am trying to decide what is different about you. Robert usually chose his women for their beauty.' Bea's start of surprise made Mrs Robinson-Fleming laugh bitterly. 'You did not think you were the only one! Where did you think he went when he left you for long periods?'

'He travelled a great deal.' Bea shrugged. 'I just assumed he went home.'

'Not to me, thank the Lord! He has, had, a more or less permanent mistress in Edinburgh but they never pretended to be married or faithful.'

Bea was beginning to understand the lady's attitude. She had been humiliated by her husband flaunting his affairs. But this was different and would cause a massive scandal. Self-defence was a very strong motive to divert blame elsewhere.

Bea wondered if she had ever known Rob at all. How many more shocks was she to receive that day?

Lady Leith had been watching Bea's reaction. The girl was shocked but still acted like a well-bred lady. She did not deserve to be punished for Robert's deceit.

'Miss Hastings, do you have family you can turn to?' Lady Leith asked gently.

'Not that I know of.'

In response to Lady Leith's questions, Bea revealed that her mother had been the daughter of Baron Conlyn, whose main estate had been in Ireland but he died before her mother married. 'Mama said he was ashamed of her infirmity and did not allow her to go into society.' When the Baron died the estate passed to a cousin. Grace was left the contents of her father's library and a small sum of money. 'My Papa was the Baron's secretary. When Mama was going to be homeless, he married her.' Bea laughed ruefully. 'That sounds familiar. I wonder if that was why he never spoke of his past. Perhaps I am not even Miss Hastings.'

'I think you can put your mind at rest on that point,' Lady Leith assured her. 'I am acquainted with a Mrs Hastings whose son fits the description of your father. Was his name John?' Bea nodded. 'Then you do have family.'

'Why did Papa never mention his family? When I was very young, I ask about his family, he just said 'not any more'. I just assumed they were all dead and that was why it made him unhappy.'

'Will you allow me to make a few enquiries on your behalf. The present Mrs Hastings is a sensible, kindly lady who, I am sure, go out of her way to help you.'

'I can't just turn up on her doorstep! There must have been a good reason for the estrangement. I don't want to involve anyone else if this gets out.'

Mrs Robinson-Fleming shuddered. 'Then you must go somewhere no-one knows you. Just disappear.'

It was a harsh judgement. Bea was of no interest to Mrs Robinson-Fleming as long as she did not cause a scandal. Having been assured that Bea agreed, Mrs Robinson-Fleming stood up to leave. She thanked Bea for the tea as though this had been a casual visit and moved towards the door.

Lady Leith was in no hurry to join her. She placed a comforting hand on Bea's arm. 'Do not despair. There is always a solution to any problem if one thinks about it clearly.'

Bea did not know whether to laugh or cry. They were almost the same words Rob had used. And look where that had got her!

'I am not helpless,' Bea assured the kind lady. 'I have run the business for over three years and have assets. I will not go begging to people I do not know.'

At the mention of assets, Mrs Robinson-Fleming turned back. 'Are they in Robert's name?'

'No. He made sure everything was legally mine. He was my friend, my Uncle Rob, who was, I thought going out of his way to help me.'

'Well, that will be a first. It was my money that set him up in business!' With no further interest, the widow opened the door and tapped her foot impatiently.

Bea escorted her visitors out to their carriage, which was drawing a lot of interest from her neighbours. She would soon be besieged by the curious and wondered what on earth to tell them.

'So that's about it,' Bea told Dora later. Freddie had been sent away after being told Rob had died. He and Dora knew of the closure notice, of course. And, like Bea, had been confident that Rob would help them find another shop. Bea had only added that the Ladies had come to inform her of Rob's sudden death.

Rob had been Freddie's hero. Bea could not tell him the more sordid facts.

It did not occur to Bea to hold anything back from Dora. Dora was closer to her than any relatives who might, or might not, wish to acknowledge her.

'I don't know what to say,' Dora declared.

'That is certainly worth recording,' Bea said with a bitter laugh.

Dora huffed, 'Get away with you!' and then joined in the laughter. She was not usually shy of giving her opinion. She sobered. 'But seriously, Bea, what are we to do now?'

'I told Lady Leith we could manage but I think she will make enquiries anyway. We must start packing and….. oh, there is so much to do. We will be gone before the 31st. I will not give Tanner the opportunity of turning us out physically.'

Chapter 5

Over the next few days Bea let it be known that her husband had died suddenly on a trip abroad. Her neighbours were practical people. They had accepted her sudden marriage as a sensible arrangement and viewed her intention of spending time at the seaside while she decided where to live permanently in the same way. The Hastings had always been respected and Bea had shown herself to be more than capable of arranging her own life. Their condolences were sincere. There were even a few hopes that Bea would let them know where she decided to settle. Bea was touched by their kindly concern and made non-committal answers. She hated lying but when she left here, she would sever all connection.

Bea was too busy to give in to her shattered feelings. She sold the entire stock to a dealer she had done business with before. He offered less than the books were worth but they both knew Bea was in no position to haggle. As a sop to his conscience he did send two of his own staff to do the packing.

Most of the furniture and household paraphernalia was sold or given to the Charity Committee to distribute to the needy.

Some things were too precious to be discarded. Her father's desk was the epitome of the person he had presented to the world at large – good quality, a bit dull and concealing more than it revealed. The bureau where her mother had spent so many hours held similar memories. Bea had often wondered how two such diverse characters had lived together happily for so many years. These and a few other items, including her piano and the family strong box, would go into storage until Bea found a place she could live quietly as an ageing spinster. It was a depressing thought but she would not be alone.

It was a given that Dora and Freddie would go with her. They had both proved their loyalty and love over the years and would probably have followed if she had tried to dismiss them.

On the 29th of March St Ann's Row was crowded with vehicles. The storage company wagon had arrived first and loaded their items but the driver said he would wait in case anything had been left behind. People who had purchased items that were needed until Bea moved came next. Then a large cart under the supervision of the vicar's wife. The shop doorway was jammed with people coming and going. Everyone wanted to linger to see Mrs Fleming on her way.

The carriage Bea had commissioned had to park further down the road. Freddie helped the driver with their personal luggage, prolonging the process by saying goodbye to his friends. Dora kept hold of a battered satchel that contained all Bea's precious documents and small items of jewellery.

'That's it,' Dora said after everything was cleared. The empty rooms looked lonely and felt suddenly cold. Freddie stood at Bea's shoulder filled with a mixture of regret and excitement. It had been his home too. He had become very protective since Rob had made a joking command to the boy to look after the ladies. He was now a strapping young man, a far cry from the skinny six-year-old Grace had taken in off the streets. Since Tanner's last visit he stuck to Bea like a bulldog.

While Bea locked the door and handed the key to a neighbour. Freddie stepped further out into the street, scanning the crowd.

'Time to go, Freddie,' Dora called. 'Who are your looking for?'

'Tanner,' Freddie replied. 'I want to give him something to remember me by.'

A fracas was the last thing Bea wanted. She owed it to her parents to make her departure as respectable as they had always lived. Secretly she would have loved to see Tanner get his come-uppance.

Taking one last look at the shuttered premises, Bea gently took the lad's arm. 'Come now. You know you can hardly wait to travel on top like a real footman.'

Freddie had just seen Bea and Dora into the coach when another, very smart carriage drew up behind them. A young man jumped down and looked around. Taking in the situation at a glance he approached Bea's vehicle.

'Beatrice? I nearly missed you!'

'Who are you?' Freddie demanded as the man went to put his head inside Bea's carriage.

'Lessing! Get out of my way. I need to speak to my cousin.'

The name meant nothing to Bea but the young man bore a marked resemblance to her Papa and knew her name.

'I am Beatrice. Why are you here?'

'Mama sent me.'

'I am sorry but I do not know what you are talking about.'

He looked nonplussed. 'I am your cousin, Michael. Michael Hastings. I have come to fetch you.' He looked around at the interested spectators. 'Is there anywhere we can talk?'

It was said in such an appealing, school-boy tone Bea decided some explanations were necessary. 'There is a small hotel just around the corner. I will speak with you there but I must be on my way soon.' Bea told the driver to take them to the hotel. He grumbled about being delayed enough already but Freddie shut the carriage door and jumped up beside him. 'You heard Mrs Fleming. Chop, chop. The sooner she sends this fellow on his way the quicker we can be on ours.'

Young as he was, Michael Hastings had no difficulty in getting a private room at the hotel. 'We will not be staying. No, we do not want refreshments either.' He turned to look at Bea, 'You don't, do you?'

Bea's surprise was turning to amusement. He was very young and acted the way Freddie did when he was excited. She did insist that Dora enter the hotel room with her. 'Oh, I suppose that's right. My sisters never go anywhere without a maid.'

It was getting more confusing by the moment. With several interruptions to clarify his rambling account, Bea managed to make out that he was Viscount Lessing. His mother had sent him a message, (I was staying with a friend in Newmarket) telling him to collect his long-lost cousin from Cambridge. He did not know how his mama had found her because she was up to her eyes with Violet's come-out.

Eventually Bea said, 'I am on my way to the coast. If you give me your mother's address, I will write to her.'

'You can't do that! Mama will have my head if I return without you.'

Bea and Dora exchanged a glance. Lady Lessing did not sound like someone they would want to meet if her son was terrified of offending her. Lady Leith had obviously been in

contact with the dragon lady who probably wanted to transport
Bea to the other side of the world.

'I was planning to go for a holiday by the coast. Where do you
live?' Bea asked, stalling for time.

'Lessing is in Oxfordshire but we are all in town for the
Season.'

'We?' Bea prompted.

Another long speech revealed 'we' referred to Michael's
mother and two sisters. (Rose was nice but she was married and
lived in Bristol so she was not with them.' Lily was alright,
mostly, but still in the schoolroom. Violet, 'I told you about her
come-out' could be difficult.)

'Please come. My carriage is very comfortable. Better than
that hired thing. I doubt it will get you to wherever it was you
wanted to go.' He was so sweet and getting so distressed Bea
consented to go to London for a short visit but insisted on
travelling in her hired carriage. She could grow very fond of
Michael but she needed to discuss things with Dora. More to the
point, her head was already buzzing with all this new information
and the thought of enduring his chatter all day was just too much.

The journey from Cambridge to London was over seventy
miles, about the same as to Felixstowe. The bank manager, who
had put Bea in touch with the cottage owner, had recommended
a quiet hotel about half-way as an overnight stop. Bea doubted
Michael had arranged accommodation half-way to London.
Would a party of four plus two drivers find vacant rooms on a
busy main road?

Bea's driver was not pleased with the change of plan. 'I don't
know what the boss will say.' Bea argued that it was about the
same distance. 'You are expected to be away for four days. What
difference can it make?' Bea left him grumbling and climbed
inside the coach.

'What do you make of all that?' Bea asked when they set off
behind Michael's carriage.' Dora's advice was not always
palatable but it was given out of love and after careful
consideration of the facts at hand.

'He is too scatty to have made it up. He reminds me of Mr
Hastings, God rest his soul. He was a lovely man but he did get
into a tangle if a stranger asked him to explain anything that

wasn't in those great books he was always reading.' Dora thought for a moment. 'What puzzles me is, well, you said Lady Leith was nice. I cannot understand why she would send you to that boy's mother.'

'She didn't refer to her friend as Lady Lessing, just Mrs Hastings. I think she was talking about an older lady, an aunt perhaps.'

'That makes sense. We can always leave if Lady Lessing is as terrible as Lady Leith's other friend. You did not give a definite date for our arrival at the cottage.' Dora chuckled. 'Him up on the box won't be pleased if he has to turn around and take you Felixstowe anyway.'

Bea glossed over the last comment. 'To be fair, Mrs Robinson-Fleming had recently lost her husband, even if he was a philanderer. To find out he was a bigamist must have been the final straw.'

It was growing dark by the time they drew up in front of a large hotel. It looked expensive. Bea started to worry about clothes. She had only packed one dress, a plain one suitable for a country inn. If they did stay here, she would have to hide in her chamber.

Michael helped Bea down from the carriage and escorted her inside. Dora followed, clutching the satchel. 'Two rooms,' Michael told the receptionist.' He turned to Bea, 'Do you want your maid to stay with you?' Bea nodded. Michael faced the receptionist again. 'There are also two drivers and a footman.'

The receptionist consulted a large ledger, shaking his head and pursing his lips. *He is going to say there are no rooms,* Bea thought. Michael slipped a small card topped with a bright coin under the corner of the book. 'Please sign here, My Lord,' the receptionist said as the coin disappeared 'Someone will see to your bags.'

Bea thought the staff must operate some kind of mental communication as the manager appeared to take them up to their rooms. Bea's room was first, large and tastefully furnished. Michael left her with a casual, 'I will come back to take you down to dinner.' Bea turned to say she would prefer to have something in her room but the door was already closing. She took a few steps forwards and saw her reflection in a full-length mirror.

She had travelled in the black two-piece costume she had purchased, ready-made, when her mother died. It sapped all colour from her tired face making her look like a middle-aged widow. Bea groaned. She had seen some of the other guests, all beautifully dressed in expensive evening wear. She was still standing there when Dora arrived, followed by a staff member carrying their over-night bags.

Dora took one look at Bea and led her to a chair. 'Just you sit there a minute.' How Dora could be so brisk amazed Bea. She was at least ten years older and been through the same traumatic events of the day.

The grey dress Bea had considered suitable for a country inn was creased and of even poorer quality than the suit. 'I can't go down in that.' Dora agreed and, after Bea had washed her face and tidied her hair, gave the suit a quick brush down. Just in time before Michael knocked on the door.

Bea was further surprised when the dining staff showed her more deference than they did Michael. They were shown to a quiet table in an alcove. It was only as she carefully scanned the room that it hit Bea. Given her appearance, Michael's obvious youth and the names recorded in the ledger the staff thought she was recently bereaved and escorted by a young relative. Hopefully not her son.

Bea forgot about the other diners as the food was served and Michael set out to entertain her. Thankfully in a more coherent manner.

'What did Lady Leith tell you?' Bea asked.

'What has she to do with anything? I just received a note from Mama saying you were coming to live with us.'

That was both a relief and a worry. From reading novels Bea had learned that distressed females were often taken in as companions or general helpers. They were never quite servants but certainly not cherished relatives. Bea was determined not to become either!

'I have a cottage waiting for me. By the seaside. I have always wanted to see the ocean.

'You can't live there alone!'

'I won't be alone. I will have Dora and Freddie.'

'You won't need them. Our house is overflowing with servants.'

Bea made it clear that Dora and Freddie were to stay with her, wherever it happened to be.

'Oh, well you can sort it out with Mama.' Having lost interest in that topic Michael asked why she wore black. 'It don't suit you.'

Bea could not help laughing. He was not being rude so she pulled a face and said, 'That is not a very polite thing to say to a lady.

'Isn't it? Violet is always telling me I don't know how to behave like a Viscount.'

'How long have you held the title?'

'Too long.' He sighed.

'It is awful to lose one's father,' Bea commiserated.

Michael frowned. 'Is it? I hardly noticed as he never spent much time with us.'

How many more pieces are there to this puzzle? Bea wondered. Too many to be coped with tonight. She said she was tired and would like to go back to her room.

Chapter 6

Next morning Michael sent a note saying they would complete the journey by train. Her luggage could follow in his carriage. Bea went along to his room as soon as she was dressed to tell him this would not do. Michael looked startled. when he opened his door and hissed, 'You can't come in here even if you are my cousin. I will see you downstairs.' The door closed in Bea's face and she felt like stamping her foot in irritation. She was not going to arrive at Lady Lessing's door with only a small bag and a creased dress. Bea stomped down the stairs to the lounge and ordered coffee for something to do while she waited.

Michael soon joined her and started with a lecture. 'Don't you know it is disaster to go to a man's room?' Of course, she did. But she was worried about their things.

'I can't turn up on your mother's doorstep with only one dress.'

Michael looked her up and down. 'Mama will find you something. You are about the same size as Violet.' He frowned. 'No, perhaps you should not ask Violet, she gets into a pet at the least little thing. But Mama is nice. She never gets upset. Every says how nice she is.'

That seemed to contradict some of his previous statements. Perhaps the boy really was addled in his wits.

Bea almost dreaded to ask about the changes to their journey.

'You will love it,' Michael assured her. 'I take the train whenever I can but there was no connection.' Bea stopped him as he launched into a recital of his journeys and escaped back to her room.

Dora greeted her with, 'That boy is so excited about going on a train.' Bea blinked before she realised Dora was referring to Freddie. 'And the driver wants to see you. He is not happy.'

Bea trailed downstairs again and out to the carriage yard. From the looks she received this was somewhere else a lady should not go.

'I am not happy,' the driver declared. 'I don't know what the boss will say. First, we trail that young sprig now he wants your things transferred to his carriage. I don't know what the boss will say about me leaving you with someone you had never met until yesterday.'

Bea didn't care what the boss said about anything. She was sorely tempted to ask to be taken to Felixstowe. In the last month her life had been turned upside down, inside out and sideways. She wanted time and space and silence, not necessarily in that order. 'Please just do as instructed. I will write to your employer.' Then it was back upstairs again to put on her hat.

Dora had done a hasty raid on their trunks and retrieved a few more essential items. The repacked bags were taken down and given to Freddie. He was also burdened with another bag that Michael assumed he would carry. That was the last she saw of Freddie or luggage until much later.

Bea and Dora enjoyed the luxury of a first-class, ladies only compartment. The other ladies looked down their noses and ignored them.

Bea was glad the journey was relatively short. Under different circumstances she would probably have been as excited as Freddie. The closer they got to London the more Bea's apprehension increased. What was she supposed to do when the train stopped? Where was Michael? Where was Freddie and their luggage? Was Lady Lessing a domestic tyrant or 'very nice'?

When the train stopped Michael was suddenly there to help her down. A little further down the platform Freddie and a porter were loading the bags onto a trolley. A uniformed footman was waiting at the barrier to show the way to two carriages waiting at the station entrance.

'How did they know to be here,' Bea asked. 'The hotel sent a telegram,' Michael replied as though it was the normal thing to do.

It was one more highlight of the way her life had changed. The Hastings had led quiet but busy lives. If anything needed doing, they generally did it themselves. Michael assumed any wish he had would be met.

As they travelled westwards the streets became wider and the houses larger. The poorly dressed pedestrians were replaced by elegant people strolling arm in arm. Bea watched it all with excitement mixed with trepidation.

The carriage stopped in a square with a fenced garden in the centre. Bea could not see the tops of the houses from the carriage but the number of windows suggested they were all very large. The footman jumped down and ran to thump on the nearest door before hurrying back to open the carriage door. Michael helped Bea down and she had her first real glance of London at its best.

A recent shower had left the pavements sparkling in the Spring sunshine. A gentle breeze carried the scent of new growth and a sprinkling of petals from the flowering trees.

Someone must have been watching for them as the front door was open and a smiling lady stood on the front step.

'Here she is, Mama.' Michael shouted. 'I nearly missed her.'

'Not on the doorstep, dear.' The lady held out her hands to Bea. 'Welcome to London, Beatrice.' She linked her arm with Bea's and drew her inside. Michael followed, giving details of their journey. 'Well done, Mickie,' Lady Lessing said over her shoulder. 'I will hear all about it later.'

The vestibule, it was too grand to be a mere hallway, took Bea's breath away. She had to stop herself from gaping at the expanse of polished floor, gilded side tables, mirrors and flowers. Closed doors on either side gave no clue to their uses. A well-dressed man took Bea's bonnet which he immediately passed on to a hovering maid. The maid beckoned to Dora and led her away into the interior of the house. Not to the wide staircase but down a side corridor. Bea watched her friend disappear with a deep sense of loss.

Her hostess led her towards the stairs. Michael had already bounded up the first flight, two steps at a time. The ladies followed more slowly allowing Bea to take in primrose walls and large portraits. A second flight turned at right angles to cross the rear of the hall allowing Bea to see the space from a different angle. She was almost at eye-level with an immense chandelier hung on a chain which drew her eyes up into a distant dome with windows to let in the light. Feeling totally bemused Bea hardly heard her hostess's continued welcome. Suddenly aware that she was expected to respond, Bea muttered an apology. 'No matter,' her hostess replied. 'I expect you would like time to freshen up.

Your maid should be waiting for you and I will send someone to show you to the drawing room for tea when you are ready.'

Bea was gracefully transferred to another maid who appeared from nowhere. A wide corridor and more stairs led to a narrower passage with doors on either side. The maid threw open a door and ushered Bea inside.

The bedroom was prettily furnished in shades of pink and white and Dora was there, a solid and comforting reminder of home.

Bea sank into a chair. 'Oh, Dora, what have I let us in for?'

'A life of ease and comfort. A bit starchy but hot water was delivered without being asked for and your bag is in the dressing room.'

'Freddie is here?'

Dora shrugged. 'Somewhere. He would not have handed over your bag and just disappeared.'

Dora's matter of fact attitude steadied Bea. 'I have just been told, very nicely, to make myself presentable before being allowed in the drawing room.'

'We had better get on with it then.' Dora showed her the dressing room and helped her to change into a dress she had rescued from their abandoned trunks. It was also black but less wrinkled. While Bea did her own hair Dora asked, 'What is the mistress like?'

'Not at all like Michael. She has blonde hair and looks much too young to be his mother but is just as friendly.' Bea giggled, 'Fortunately she does not talk so much. She seems pleased to see me and said she was glad to meet me at last.'

There was a knock on the door. Dora went to answer it and allowed a young girl who resembled Lady Lessing to enter. 'Hello. I am Lily, Michael's youngest sister. Mama sent me to fetch you.' Bea guessed she was around eleven or twelve years old with a friendly smile and the same buzz of vitality as her brother

'How do you do? Michael said I would like you.'

Lily's smile lit up her whole face. 'Oh, good. Are you ready to go down? I am allowed to join you and there will be cake.'

Bea remembered reading that young girls were kept in the schoolroom. Being allowed to take tea in the drawing room was a treat.

'I never knew about you until a few days ago,' Lily confided as they made their way down some of the stairs.

'I did not know about you, either. I understand you have two sisters?'

Lily nodded. 'Rose is lovely but Violet is... Well, the season has gone to her head.' Whatever that meant was not clear but they had reached the drawing room. Lady Lessing invited Bea to sit beside her on a velvet sofa.

Before she sat down Bea said, 'Thank you for inviting me, Lady Lessing. It was quite unexpected.'

Mother and daughter both laughed. 'I am not Lady Lessing. Just plain Mrs Hastings.'

'Papa never held the title,' Lily chipped in

'It is rather complicated,' Mrs Hastings said, 'but it can wait until we have had our tea. Ah, here it is now.'

Two maids appeared through one of the panelled walls, carrying trays. While they arranged the silver tea service and china Bea had a chance to look around. The overall impression was of a scene frozen in time. The panelling, the shape of the windows and even the furniture bore the stamp of early Georgian architecture.

'Grim isn't it.'

Bea snapped her attention back to Mrs Hastings. It would be rude to agree but Mrs Hastings only laughed. 'I have not yet had time to redecorate the whole house. We are only using this room in honour of your arrival.'

Bea was saved from making any reply as Lily stood up to pass Bea a cup of tea and a small plate. With both hands full Bea wondered what she was to do with either until a silent maid placed a small table at her side. Bea had barely set down her cup before Lily was back, wafting a selection of dainty cakes under her nose. 'Please say you do not care for cream horns. They are my favourite.'

'Lily!' Mrs Hastings said sharply. 'Whatever will Beatrice think of your manners?' The words were censorious but Mrs Hastings was smiling. She turned to Bea. 'We are all still learning how to behave as Society expects.' Seeing Bea's confusion, she added, 'Don't worry about it now. Drink your tea and please take the cream horn if you wish.' Mother and daughter pulled faces at each other and Bea was instantly at ease.

Mrs Hastings was not a dragon. She knew how to correct her children but it was done gently. It was so reminiscent of her own Mama Bea wanted to cry.

But it also added to her confusion. Everything she saw and heard was contradicted a moment later. From the moment she met him, Michael had seemed an odd sort of Viscount. He had held the title for several years but the family did not know how to behave in the way Society expected. Bea had been afraid her own lack of Society experience would make her an embarrassment. Everything she knew came from books which were probably out of date. Her Mother's advice had been to treat every individual, whether king or commoner, with respect and politeness.

Bea was not allowed to ponder the questions for long. Mrs Hastings had turned the conversation into casual enquiries about Bea's journey and did she have everything she needed in her room.

Bea mentioned her lack of suitable clothing. She had only packed clothes suitable for settling into at a quiet cottage. Most of her dresses were black or dark grey as she had not bothered with fashion since her mother died. All her best clothes had been sent into storage with the furniture.

Bea put her cup down on the table. 'Lady… ah, Mrs Hastings, it was very kind of you to invite me but you must not think I mean to impose.'

'It is no imposition. I never met your parents but John was clearly my mother-in-law's favourite. How much did Lady Leith tell you about the family?'

'Very little. She only mentioned a past friendship.' Bea smiled. 'I was expecting a much older lady.'

Mrs Hastings nodded. 'She was a close friend of my mother-in-law in their earlier years. I am glad she came to me. I have often wondered what my husband's twin brother was like.' Bea's start of surprise drew an answering frown of enquiry.

'I did not know Papa had a brother. When I was very young, I asked him if he had a family and he said 'not now'. I assumed they were all dead and that was what made him too sad to talk about them.'

'It is sad. It has taken a tragedy to bring you back to us.'

'What did Lady Leith tell you about me?'

Mrs Hastings glanced quickly at her avidly listening daughter. 'Just that she met you by chance when your situation had suddenly changed.'

Bea breathed a sigh of relief. Mrs Hastings knew more than she was willing to say in front of her daughter. How much more would have to wait until they could talk privately.

Mrs Hastings changed the subject. 'Did Mickie tell you he has three sisters?'

Before Bea could reply, Lily said, 'I told her about Violet and Rose.' She bit her lips and looked at her Mama before adding, 'Just their names.'

Another mystery. Michael had barely mention Rose apart from saying she was married and lived in Bristol.

The tense moment passed when there came the sound of approaching footsteps. 'That must be Violet returning from her visit,' Mrs Hastings said quickly. Lily groaned.

The door burst open and a very pretty girl rushed half way across the room before she noticed Bea. 'You have arrived then.'

Mrs Hastings stood up. 'Violet, come and meet your cousin Beatrice.' Her voice was calm but it held a strong reprimand.

They exchanged conventional greetings, cool on Violet's side and puzzled on Bea's.

Violet had her mother's beautiful features but her hair was more golden and dressed into ringlets that bounced as she moved. She was wearing a smart ensemble of jade green which echoed the colour of her eyes. Eyes that surveyed Bea with hostility and contempt.

'I was about to explain to Beatrice that I would have to leave her alone this evening while we attend Lady Sheen's soiree.'

Violet gave Bea another raking glance. 'Well, you can hardly take her……. uninvited.' The last was an accusation. Violet plainly thought Bea unworthy of mixing with her betters.

'That was rude!' Lily said. Mrs Hastings raised a hand to silence her and turned back to Bea. 'It is a prearranged appointment. As your luggage has not arrived, we will not change for dinner.'

'May I come down too,' Lily asked eagerly. Two 'No's', one a parental decision, the other and expression of horror, made Lily pout but she did not argue.

Mrs Hastings continued. 'When we are alone, I prefer to use the morning room. The formal dining room still intimidates me.' Bea doubted anything – or anyone – was capable of intimidating her hostess. Small she might be but she was definitely in control.

'Well, I hope dinner is early. I need time to dress.' The combined emphasis on 'I' and another look at Bea spoke volumes.

'Then you may go and make your initial preparations now,' Mrs Hastings tone made it sound like a dismissal. Violet flushed and flounced towards the door. As she passed Lily's chair, she found another target. 'What are you doing here? Get back to the schoolroom where you belong.'

'Violet!' This time Mrs Hastings did not try to hide her anger.

Lily smirked and was told, more quietly, 'Run along now. You will have time to get to know Beatrice later.'

The girls left the room. Bea could hear them arguing even through the closed door.

Mrs Hastings sat down again. 'I am sorry about that.'

'My Papa said you cannot take responsibility for other people's actions.'

'That is generous of you. I do not know what has got into Violet lately. It is not the way she has been brought up. They really do love each other but sisters do bicker. You have been spared that, at least.'

'I would have liked a sister or brother. Michael and Lily already feel like family.'

'Of course, they do. You are closely related but still have much to catch up on.'

That brought Bea back to a previous question. 'What did Lady Leith really tell you about me?'

Mrs Hastings moved to a chair closer to Bea and took hold of her hand. 'A great deal that I have not and will not mention to another soul. I never met the man I refuse to name but my mother-in-law always spoke fondly of him and would be appalled at his behaviour.'

'Then that makes it even kinder of you to invite me into your family.' Bea was close to tears.

'It is your family by blood, my connection is only through marriage. We have very little time at the moment but I will give you a few facts. My late husband was your father's twin brother. Mickie inherited the title from his great grandfather, all the intervening males having died. You have two great aunts and some other cousins but they rarely visit Lessing or come to town. I am sorry I have to leave you alone this evening as you must have lots of questions.' She took Bea's nod as agreement and went on. 'There is a family tree in the library you can study.' She laughed, 'That should really make you feel at home.'

Mrs Hastings showed Bea the library before they went to their own rooms.

Dora was waiting for Bea and looking rather worried. 'I went to find Freddie to warn him not to chatter. But, as he does not know the whole truth, he had already mentioned that you were recently widowed. The servants are curious, of course, but I think they are loyal. They are also guarding some secret.'

'I gained the same impression.'

'That does not concern us. Your cat is out of the bag and we need to stop it running wild.'

The disastrous affair was never far from Bea's mind. She had already decided to keep her visit as short as possible and then disappear again.

'Mrs Hastings is so kind but I do not know exactly how she has explained my sudden appearance. Oh, I ought not to have come here. We will have to leave tomorrow.'

A light tap on the door and Mrs Hastings slipped inside. 'We will have to be quick but we need to align our stories.'

'I will leave.'

'No, that will cause too much comment. This is what I propose.'

Mrs Hastings was a quick thinker. She had made Bea's arrival sound like a big surprise. All anyone else knew was that Bea had been in danger of losing her home. Now word of her marriage had slipped out they had to come up with a plausible reason.

'I suggest we let it be known that you are a recent widow but your marriage was so unhappy you cannot talk about it and wish to be known by your maiden name. It means I cannot take you about just yet but we will not hide you away.'

'Mrs Hastings, I do not know how to thank you.'

'There is no need. You are innocent. You have been treated abominably and I will not see you suffer for it.'

Bea tried to thank her again and was stopped with a spontaneous hug. 'And I think we can dispense with the Mrs Hastings. You must call me Jane.'

The dinner gong prevented them from saying more. Jane waited while Bea wiped away her tears and then escorted her down to dinner.

Dinner was not the ordeal Bea had expected. I was just the three ladies as Michael had gone out. Jane and Bea's natural good manners glossed over Violet's rudeness by allowing the girl to do most of the talking. Violet bragged about her social success, her clothes and planned activities. She was not actually rude, just disdainful. Bea knew she was poorly dressed but that had been explained by her lack of luggage. It was Violet's condescending manner that really annoyed Bea.

Bea thought it a pity they could not be friends. She had taken to the rest of the family on first meeting. Violet was a younger version of her beautiful Mama but her expression was often spoilt by her petulance. From various comments Bea thought this was not her usual behaviour. Something was worrying Violet and Bea wondered if it was at the root of the caution Dora had detected in the servants.

Bea tried a tentative approach by admiring Violet's elegant clothes and saying she would seek Violet's advice when she came out of mourning. A few more details were enough to send Violet off with enough gossip to make her the centre of attention at the party.

Chapter 7

Bea spent the rest of the evening in the library. It was as sombre as the drawing room with pride of place given to a large portrait the seventh Viscount Lessing. He wore a powdered wig so Bea could not see his natural hair colour but he had the same shaped face and features as her father. Only the eyes were different, dark and assessing and seemed to follow her when she moved. Bea turned her back on him and went to examine the illuminated family tree. It was impressive with gold frame, scrolling and a coat of arms. Bea frowned as she searched for her own name but it was not there. Her father was only mentioned by his date of birth.

What had happened for him to be cut off so completely? She found a pencil and some paper and sketched out a few details as she would never remember all the names.

The tree began with George, the Seventh Viscount born in 1765, married to Maria Colt in 1787 and died in 1859. Two sons had predeceased their father, the eldest without issue. The second son also had two sons, Albert and John with the same date of birth in 1819. Albert had died two years before his father. Albert was Michael's father.

There were also several female children along the line but they were ignored after the date of their marriages.

Bea kept going back to her father's name. From what she could remember, her Papa had been unhappy about not having a family. She could not believe he had done anything to deserve being cut off. Which raised the question – Had **He** cut them out of **his** life? She would have to wait until she could ask Jane.

It was getting late and Bea had no idea what time the others would return. She roamed the shelves hoping the touch and smell of the books would restore some semblance of her former, peaceful life. Bea laughed at her stupid wish and went to up bed.

'There was no need for you to wait up,' Bea told Dora when she entered her bedroom. Dora got up from her seat and made Bea a mock curtsey. 'I have been instructed on how a lady's maid should behave.'

Servants' dinner had supplied Dora with a lot of useful knowledge and some very impertinent comments.

'Parker, Miss Violet's maid, who likes to be referred to as a dresser, threw up her hands in horror when I forgot to call you Miss Hastings - ''Or should that be Mrs Something?'' she dared to add. The butler rapped on the table and frowned at her.'

Dora approved of Sampson, the butler. Mrs Duncan, the housekeeper had been with Mrs Hastings for many years when they lived in the country. She had assigned Daisy, a very young maid, to wait on them. 'What do you think of that? A lady's maid does not carry up the hot water or empty the slops. But I think she has been set up as a spy.'

'Surely not!'

'It is what I would do if a mysterious, long-lost member of a family suddenly put in an appearance. A more experienced girl would ask leading questions, putting us on our guard. Daisy is so pumped up at the promotion she will disarm us and report back, also out of ignorance.'

That sat uncomfortably with Bea. An incautious word from either of them could expose the whole family to scandal. 'We have to leave,' Bea said again. 'Perhaps not tomorrow but very soon. Jane has been so kind I will not risk harming her, or her children.'

Dora grinned. 'Every plan can backfire. Daisy, by her very nervousness at any mention of the family, confirms that the Hastings are teetering on the brink of their own scandal.'

'Oh, I want to go home,' Bea wailed and then swallowed a sob. 'But the cottage will be the next best thing.'

POSSIBLE CHAPTER BREAK HERE

The next morning Dora informed Bea that the ladies of the house took breakfast in bed. Lily had hers in the schoolroom and the Viscount rode out early and ate later. She had already ordered Bea's usual breakfast which Daisy would bring up soon.

'I am not ill. I will get up and dress now.'

Daisy brought up her breakfast and Dora went back downstairs with her. Eating breakfast did not take long and Bea wondered what to do next. Boredom was a new experience as she was not used to being idle. The last few days had been tiring because she had spent them travelling or sitting around talking.

She needed exercise. Her bedroom overlooked a strip of garden that continued around the other side of the house. She longed to explore but it was raining. It would not normally have deterred her but she thought walking in the rain was something else ladies were not expected to do.

She took out one of the novels she had kept back from the book sales and tried to read. But it did not hold her attention. She already knew the story having read The Pickwick Papers when it was published in instalments. She closed the book and took out the sketch she had made of the family tree as though studying it again would answer all the questions buzzing around in her head. Bea tucked it into her pocket and decided to go back to the library for another look at the original. Not expecting the room to be occupied at this early hour, Bea walked in without knocking. Three startled faces turned in her direction and the three men got to their feet.

'Bea!' Michael cried out joyfully and rushed forward to take her hand.

A discreet cough remined him of his manners and he introduced Bea to Lord Ashley and Mr Soames, two of his former guardians. They were both elderly and looked none too pleased by the intrusion. Bea started to back away with apologies but Michael said, 'You were left alone last evening I hear. Let me show you around.'

The men and Bea all protested with varying degrees of politeness but Michael said he would see his visitors later and ushered Bea from the room. 'Escape,' he said gleefully when the door was closed. 'What would you like to do first?'

Michael's freedom was short lived. They were only half way across the front hall when they saw Jane coming towards them.

'Mickie? I thought you were seeing Lord Ashley and Mr Soames this morning.'

Michael muttered something under his breath. 'Good morning, Mama. 'I was just…..'

'Absconding,' Jane finished for him. 'Michael Hastings, the gentlemen have given up a great deal of time on your behalf. I will take care of Beatrice so you can re-join them.'

Red to the tips of his ears, Michael murmured an apology and returned to the library.

From something Michael had said during one of his ramblings, Bea knew he had been kept from any involvement in his affairs until he reached his majority. He had complained about now being expected to learn so much about his inheritance it made his head ache. Bea thought the gentlemen's time would have been better spent in short periods over a number of years.

Jane shook her head. 'I keep forgetting he is of age.'

'It must be difficult for Michael, too. He did mention being denied any involvement until now.'

'A mistake I argued with more than once. I was told, firmly but politely, not to interfere.'

As they talked, Jane had led Bea to the morning room. It overlooked another aspect of the garden which looked inviting even in the rain.

'This is my favourite room,' Jane said and Bea could understand why. It faced east and would be delightful on a sunny morning. Even now it was light and feminine and furnished with pieces more in tune with Jane's personality. They made themselves comfortable and Jane said, 'I can see you are bursting with questions. Where do you want to start?'

Bea took out her sketch of the family tree. She wanted to ask about her father but thought she would get some background knowledge first.

'The Seventh Viscount was very old when he died.'

'Ninety-four and in total control until the moment he died.'

The more Bea heard about her great-grand-father the less she liked him. He had been autocratic and secretive. His business affairs were dealt with by a number of different secretaries and lawyers so no one person knew the extent of his holdings until he died. But he was not mean with money. His sons were educated at the best schools and then given a generous allowance and encouraged to spend their lives in selfish pleasure. His daughters were given large dowries and married off at a young age.

'The trustees were only carrying out their last instructions,' Jane said. 'In fairness, it did take them a long time to unravel and understand everything themselves.'

'I don't think I would have liked him,' Bea said.

Jane laughed. 'I don't think anyone did. I don't think he liked anyone either, He just enjoyed having everyone on a string.

When we were all called to an assembly,' Jane shook her head. 'I cannot think of any other way to describe it. It was not a celebration. In fact a summons could arrive at any time. As I was saying, when we all assembled, he looked us over, made a few comments and then sent us away again.'

'He sounds very odd,' Bea remarked.

Jane agreed. 'He was a contemporary of old George the Third and he was very eccentric too.'

Their discussion paused while they were served coffee and tiny biscuits. Jane might say she was unfamiliar with society manners but she was very adept at separating serious matters from refreshment. She talked about the weather and her plans for the garden. They compared books they had read and favourite foods. It was all very civilised.

The coffee tray was removed and Bea launched in with the topic she most wanted to discuss. 'How much do you know about my Papa?'

'Only what I have been told by my Mother-in-law, a lovely lady and the male members of the family. Opinions differ. I will have to go back to set the scene.'

Mrs Hastings senior had been married at an early age to a man she did not know and later came to despise for his hedonistic lifestyle. She had tried to raise her sons in a different mould but Albert, Jane's husband took after his grandfather. 'Ours was not a happy marriage,' Jane said sadly. Albert had taken Holy Orders, as it was an appropriate occupation for a member of the junior branch of the family but left his parish in the care of a curate, his wife and children on a small country estate and proceeded to drink himself to death.

'It is not a pretty story, is it?' Jane asked when she finished that episode. 'I have never disparaged my husband to the children but Mickie heard things at school and there are some people in society who like nothing better than to see others humiliated.'

'My Papa was not like that,' Bea insisted.

Jane touched her hand. 'I know and that is the root of the problem.'

Bea listened, alternately sickened and proud. John Hastings had also studied for the priesthood but he was shy, was inclined to stammer and dreaded being in the public eye. He had refused to become a priest and found work for himself as secretary to a politician.

'My maternal grandfather,' Bea confirmed. 'Mama told me how they met and married.'

Jane nodded. 'I am afraid the next bit might upset you.'

Bea prepared for the worst. 'The old Viscount might have let the career change pass but John compounded his offence by marrying without his grandfather's consent.' Jane squeezed Bea's hand. 'Oh, my dear, your mother's disability was the final straw.'

'That is why Papa was banished? Because he married the lady he loved so much he faded away after she died?'

'It was not quite like that. The Viscount did not disinherit John. He refused to acknowledge your mother and forbade John to bring her into society. My husband agreed with the decision. John chose to take his wife away from insult and cut himself off from his family. I am afraid that is a very diluted account.'

What Jane had said about differing opinions was now clear. Her grandmother had called John her favourite. The male contingent had seen John as weak because he was shy. An embarrassment because he stuttered, not that Bea had ever heard him do so but he did get flustered. And stupid for marrying a cripple.

'What arrogance! What right did they have to condemn Mama without getting to know what a brave and wonderful person she was!' Bea's tears were more from anger. 'Oh, I wish they were not dead! I would have something to say to them!'

Jane was equally crying and laughing with her. 'I do believe you would! I wish I had known about you earlier. And Your parents.'

'My Mama was not a cripple,' Bea continued indignantly. 'The weakness in her left side did not prevent her from living a full and useful life. I never realised how strong my Papa was to stand up to that, that Tyrant! And neither of them ever said a word about how they had been treated. I am so proud of them.' Bea started to cry again. But they were healing tears. Love and courage had conquered spite.

Jane gathered the weeping girl into her arms until she was called away to deal with a domestic crisis.

Left alone, Bea mulled over what is had heard. It explained so much. Her father's sadness at, presumable, being denied access to his mother. Her mother's occasional comments about being a perfect lady when Bea had done something wrong. She had done everything she could to prepare Bea for her rightful place in society and at the same time ensured she had the knowledge and financial support to live an independent life.

Bea remembered that Jane had also suffered from the Hastings' biased attitude. She had been pushed aside while her husband enjoyed himself. No wonder she did not feel she was prepared to face Society.

Bea frowned. Jane was prepared. She was strong enough to take Bea in despite the threatened scandal. And again, there was something in the present Hastings family that was not talked about.

Bea could not place a double burden on her new friend's shoulders. She would leave before anything leaked out. And it would eventually. No secret was secure if it was known to more than one person.

Bea dried her tears and wandered over to the long window. It reached almost to the floor with sashes that could be raised to allow one to step outside. The rain had stopped and weak sunlight sparkled on the wet grass. Bea thought whimsically that her storm of tears had even emptied the clouds. It was the sort of thing her father would have said. Instead of sadness, the thought of her Papa filled her with courage. She would not shame his memory by feeling sorry for herself.

Bea was reaching up to unlock the window when the door opened behind her. She turned with a smile, ready to assure Jane that she had recovered her spirits. But it was Violet. She was wearing a loose afternoon dress of printed cotton which should have looked casual but Violet's poise made it seem fit for a ball.

Violet stayed in the doorway and looked around the room. 'Oh, I thought Mama was in here.'

'Jane had to go to see the housekeeper.'

Violet eyed Bea's red nose and puffy eyelids with distaste. 'You had better go and do something with your face before luncheon.' Violet's words had more than one meaning. She did not need to actually say that Bea looked a mess and implied that whatever was done to her face it would still fall short. She turned to leave saying over her shoulder, 'Your trunks have arrived. I hope you have something less depressing than dreary black.'

Another inuendo! Violet did not expect any of Bea's clothes to be worth looking at. It was true but Bea was not going to dismissed so abruptly. 'Thank you,' she called to the girl's retreating back. 'One never wants to wear the same dress two days running.' The hitch in Violet's step told Bea her shot had found its target. *Naughty!* Bea's inner voice whispered but she was smiling as she went up to change.

Dora and Daisy were in Bea's dressing room. They had made a start on unpacking the trunks and several garments were spread over the bed and chair. Dora appeared when she heard the bedroom door close, took one look at Bea and rushed forward. 'What have they done to you?' she said as Bea fell into her arms. She wasn't crying but it was comforting to be held in familiar arms. 'If it was that....' Dora remembered Daisy and called, 'Daisy, you can take the blue gown down to be pressed but don't try doing it yourself.'

The wide-eyed maid stared at the spectacle of a lady in her maid's arms until Dora told her sharply to get on with it. Daisy scuttled away eager to share her news.

Bea pulled herself upright and smiled. 'I am not upset anymore. I don't have time to tell you everything now but Papa cut himself off from the family when they would not accept Mama.'

Dora nodded and Bea frowned. 'You don't seem very surprised.'

'No, your Ma told me lots of things before she died.'

'And you did not tell me! Even when you knew I was worried!'

Dora gave her a stern look. 'Why do you trust me with your secrets?'

Shame washed colour into Bea's pale cheeks. 'I am sorry, Dora. Did Mama ask you not to tell me?'

'Only when you needed to know. And don't shake your head at me, miss! If your parents didn't want to influence you against the family, well, enough said. Now this dress is just about fit to wear and you said we do not have much time.' Dora turned away and grabbed the first garment that came to hand. Her gesture made them both laugh when she realised it was a petticoat.

Bea looked almost her normal, composed self when she joined the others in the morning room. A cold compress, some cucumber lotion and a light dusting of powder had repaired most of the damage. The grey gown was almost a replica of the one it had replaced. It was a few years out of date but could not be faulted for quality or fit. No-one needed to know that it was one she had often worn in the bookshop.

'What will madam Violet have to say about this one?' Bea asked her reflection in the mirror as she left the room.

Violet was too busy arguing with Lily to take any notice of Bea as she joined Jane at a round table had not noticed before. A soup tureen, a basket of bread rolls and small bowls were already set out. A covered plate and a fruit bowl waited on the buffet.'

'We serve ourselves at midday,' Jane said as she ladled out the soup. Lily had abandoned her argument in favour of nourishment and came to pass a bowl to Bea.

'Have you been crying?' she asked softly. 'If it was,' Lily glared across at her sister who shrugged and picked up her napkin.

Bea squeezed the girl's arm and smiled. 'I am alright now.'

Lily took the chair at right angles to Bea with Violet on her other side. Violet gave a sharp cry and said, 'She kicked me! The little beast! She should not be allowed to join us if she cannot behave.'

'Girls!' Jane intervened. 'Stop this instant. I don't know what is wrong with you lately but I have had enough of it. Behave or you will both,' she stressed with a look at Violet, 'be eating all your meals in the schoolroom.' An uneasy peace carried them through the rest of the meal. It was not silent, just held to neutral topics. Lily was more than ready to fill any gaps. Lily carried their used dishes to the sideboard and came back with the basket of fruit and plate of fruit tartlets. She offered them to her mother and then Bea. Re-taking her seat she happened to glance out of the window and said, 'It looks as though it might rain again.'

Violet was sitting with her back to the window. She twisted round and said, worriedly, 'I do hope not. You haven't forgotten we are driving with Mrs Johnson and Celia have you Mama? I will have to tell Parker to lay out my matching jacket.'

Jane reached out to take a few more grapes. 'No, Violet, I have not forgotten. I will be in the hall at half past three as arranged. I am sorry, Beatrice, that I have to leave you again.'

'I have to stay home and do my piano practice this afternoon,' Lily complained.

'Perhaps I could join you. If your Mama agrees,' Bea offered.

'You play the piano!' Violet sounded insultingly surprised.

'Yes. Not outstandingly but my parents appreciated my efforts.'

'Do you have any other accomplishments?'

Bea was tired of her cousin's sniping. She replied as blandly as she could. 'If you mean can I paint or do exquisite embroidery, then no. But I have run a successful business for more than three years'

'I hope you will not voice that abroad!'

Violet's alarm gave Bea a moment of unholy satisfaction. Beside her, Jane tensed ready to intervene. Bea smiled and shook her head. She could fight her own battles and perhaps now was the right time to make her intentions clear.

Looking directly at Violet, Bea said, 'As a recent widow, I will not be moving in society. I only came for a short visit to meet my Papa's family.'

'Oh, please don't leave,' Lily cried with real feeling.'

'Beatrice must do as she pleases. Taking a little time to adjust is not unreasonable and we will have to make her stay here so enjoyable she will want to visit us again.'

'I still don't think it is fair that Violet goes out all the time and I have to do lessons. I hardly ever see you.'

'Don't exaggerate, Lily. We have as many meals as possible together and I did warn you I would be mostly occupied with Violet's come-out.'

'I feel very guilty about taking up your time,' Bea said quietly. I did not realise I would be taking you away from your other commitments

'Oh, please don't leave,' Lily said again. 'You can share my time with Mama.'

'I only came for a visit,' Bea insisted.

'But where will you go. Mama said you had suddenly lost your home.'

'I have a small property waiting for me by the seaside.' If that implied that she owned the cottage, Bea did not care. It was only rented at the moment but came with an option to buy.

'We will all be sorry to see you go. But not too soon. You are very welcome to stay for as long as you wish.' Jane's quiet statement held regret, acceptance of Bea's decision and a warning to Violet.

As soon as the meal was finished, Violet went away to change and Lily was sent up to the drawing room. 'You can practice a few scales until Beatrice joins you.'

With her daughters safely out of earshot Jane took Bea's hand. 'I wish you did not have to leave but I can see it is necessary. Even in one day you have been forced to reveal details of your past. Please take care what you say to Lily. She will mean her questions kindly but I think it is beyond her to keep a secret.'

Bea kept that advice firmly in mind as she entered the drawing room. Lily was not there. Nor was there a piano. Bea turned right around as though girl and piano might have appeared whilst she was not looking.

The mystery was solved when Lily opened one of the wall panels. 'Through here. These walls fold back when there is a big party.' She huffed out a breath. 'That will be for Violet's ball and I won't be allowed to go to that either.'

'Your turn will come,' Bea reassured her.

'Did you have a come-out ball?'

Careful, Bea's inner voice cautioned. 'No. And it is something else I do not wish to talk about. Can you play a duet?' Bea went over the piano and started sorting through the sheets of music. 'Do you know this one?' she asked, holding out a simple two-part ballad. They played, together and singly, for more than an hour, sometimes singing and often laughing.

Bea felt sad that she was to have so little time with Lily and Jane. She had often wondered what it would be like to have a sister. Now she knew and it would break her heart to leave them.

After Bea and Lily had tea in the school room they went out into the garden. Lily fetched a ball from a small shed and threw it to Bea who missed catching it. Bea picked up the ball and threw it back but her aim was as bad as her catching. 'I bet no-one ever wants you on their team,' Lily laughed.

It was another pitfall. There had never been a team to join. Bea managed to avoid a direct answer. 'I have always been a butter-fingers. I am much better at arranging flowers. Your Mama was telling me what would be blooming here later in the year.'

Lily, with only a little prompting, described the gardens where they had lived before Michael came of age. It sounded delightful. The girls had all gone to the village school but Michael was sent away to school when he was only seven years' old. 'We did get a governess later but I liked being with other children.' Lily then asked about Bea's schooling and she had to admit that she had been taught by her parents.

'Even your father?' Lily exclaimed in surprise. 'I don't remember my father but I am sure he never had much to do with any of the others.'

Bea thought how lucky she had been to have such wonderful parents. Although, from what Jane had disclosed, Lily's father was not a very great loss.

'What are you thinking about? I asked you twice if you liked gardening.'

'Sorry. Your house and garden sounded so nice I thought I would plant the same things at my cottage.'

'What is it like?'

'I have never actually been there. But I am looking forward to seeing the ocean.'

That was enough to set Lily off again with stories about her own visits to the coast and lasted until Jane and Violet returned.

Violet was in a much better mood at dinner. They, Violet and Jane, had been invited to attend an impromptu picnic the next day. She talked, almost non-stop about what she would wear, hopes that the weather would hold and, most importantly, who would be there. 'I might meet the man I will marry.'

Michael, who had joined them for dinner, scoffed. 'What is wrong with all the men you have met already? If you are not careful you will get a reputation as a flirt.'

Bea had not seen much of Michael since her arrival. He was either with his trustees or out and about with friends. He offered to take Bea out the next day but she used the excuse of her mourning to politely refuse. He did not seem unduly disappointed.

After the meal Jane and Bea lingered at the table after the others left. 'Thank you for entertaining Lily.'

'I enjoyed it. She is very bright and I had to keep your warning in mind. She is so artless it would have been easy to let slip things she is better off not knowing.'

'I hardly dare ask you to spend more time with her tomorrow. She feels very left out and irritates Violet for something to do. I wish I had not given Miss Morrison such a long holiday.'

As they walked up the stairs Jane stopped at the first turn. 'That is my mama-in-law with her two boys when they were young.'

Bea studied the picture. It was more informal than the other portraits dotted around the house. It showed a seated lady with her head tilted down so her face was in profile. She had her arms around the two boys. The family resemblance was so strong one of the boys might have been Michael. The artist had managed to capture an ambience of tenderness.

'Which one is my papa?' Bea asked softly.

'The one who is smiling up at his mother. Look at Albert, he seems to be pulling away.'

Bea feasted her eyes on the smiling boy. It was easy to superimpose maturity and see an image of her father. She tried to memorise every detail. She had a miniature of her mama but the only remaining personal connection to her papa was the manuscript he had been working on before her mother died.

Jane allowed her time before saying, 'A portrait of the Seventh Viscount used to hang here. Lord of all he surveyed. The first time Lily saw it she said it frightened her.'

Bea could only agree if it was the picture hanging in the library. It had unnerved her as the eyes seemed to follow wherever she stood in the room.

'I know it sounds silly,' Jane laughed, 'but I whisper hello mama every time I pass.

Bea looked closer at the lady. 'Hello grandmama' she said, wishing she had been able to meet her.

When they reached Bea's bedroom door Jane gave her a hug. 'I am sorry you have to leave soon but I understand why. I will miss you.'

Bea returned the hug. 'I will miss you too. Under different circumstances I think we could have been friends.'

'We are friends,' Jane insisted. 'We will keep in touch and perhaps, someday, we will be able to spend more time together'

Bea kissed Jane cheek and entered the room before she could cry.

Chapter 8

After Jane and Violet left for the Saturday picnic Lily complained, 'Violet has all the fun.'

'Your turn will come.' Bea gave the girl a hug. 'What would you like to do today?'

'May we go shopping? Lily asked eagerly. 'The sun is shing and it is too nice to stay indoors.'

Bea was reluctant to leave the house but she understood Lily's frustration. 'Perhaps not to the shops,' she said, about to suggest the garden. Lily's glum expression made Bea reconsider. 'We could go for a walk,' she suggested as an alternative. That should be safe enough. Lily was too young to have many acquaintances in town who would want to stop and talk.

Forgetting to call for Dora to help her, Bea went to change into her black dress and jacket. With a plain bonnet hiding most of her face Bea thought she looked like a governess. She laughed at her reflection in the mirror. Actually, that would not be a bad impression. She remembered Michael saying the girls were always escorted by a maid or footman when they went out. Surely a governess fell into the same category. She had seen governesses and children in the square's central gardens. No-one would take any notice of them.

Even so, Bea gave a sigh of relieve when the footman who let them out of the front door did not comment on them going out alone.

Bea enjoyed Lily's cheerful chatter as they walked along the street but, in governess mode, did have to remind Lily not to talk so loudly. ''That is what Miss Morrison is always telling me,' Lily giggled. 'And not to gallop!'

It was a safe topic and Bea encouraged Lily to talk about her governess and her lessons. Lily was bright and intelligent, just too full of energy to be confined. In the country, Bea was told, Lily was allowed to run and shout as much as she liked but it was a bit lonely now Violet had decided to be a lady.

Bea thought of her own lonely girlhood. She had not realised it at the time. Well, only occasionally. She had loved her lessons with Mama and Papa but she also had freedom to choose how she spent the rest of her time. It was only now that she had left Cambridge that she saw how much she had missed.

They had reached the park and Lily wanted to go inside. There were not many people about as it was still too early for the fashionable parade but Bea kept them away from the carriage drive.

Bea did not know how long they had been out but the sun was high overhead and she suggested they return for lunch. They had just reached the park gates when they had to pause to allow a carriage to enter.

The lady passenger leaned forward and stared. Bea quickly lowered her head and urged Lily to walk on. Of all the bad luck. There were millions of people in London and she had to come face to face with the most notorious gossip in Cambridge.

Bea tried not to panic. Mrs Blakesby might not have recognised her. The encounter had only taken a few seconds before the carriage was past. It was easy to mistake a stranger for someone one knew.

'Are you feeling alright, Bea?' Lily asked, jerking Bea out of her worried thoughts. 'You look very pale.'

'Just a little tired,' Bea replied. 'I have overdone the exercise after days of sitting around.'

In truth she was feeling sick and wanted to hide in her room but that would make Lily more curious. They had lunch together and whiled away the afternoon playing the piano and card games, had tea and, although Bea enjoyed Lily's company, she was glad when it was time for the girl to get ready for bed.

Lily kissed her cheek and thanked her for a lovely day. 'I wish you did not have to leave. I will miss you.' There were tears in Lily's eyes as she obediently followed the housekeeper.

'Good night, my dear. I shall see you in the morning.' Bea called after her. She was also close to tears. For different reasons both sisters had almost made her cry. 'I never cry,' Bea muttered as she went to her room. Well, not very often. Learning about her father's history had been a shock. When he died, she had been too busy to give in to her grief and confusion.

'What's happened now?' Dora asked. She had been preparing a lecture about Bea dressing herself but that was forgotten.

'I saw Mrs Blakesby in the park.'

Bea told her friend about the chance meeting. 'It was so quick and she has no way of finding me. Oh, Dora, I will be glad to get away.'

Jane and Violet had not returned so Bea asked for a light meal in the morning room. It would look too odd if she said she did not feel like eating. She forced down the soup and omelette and pocketed the peach, hopefully to eat later.

Michael came in and talked about a party he was going to and said how sorry he was that Bea had decided to leave so soon. Bea did not want to talk about her reason for leaving and was trying to find an excuse to go to bed but it was only a little after nine o'clock.

The door opened to admit Violet, looking like a girl who had thoroughly enjoyed her day. Her usual perfection was blurred by tousled hair and a wrinkled dress. But her rosy cheeks and wide smile added genuine charm. Violet flopped into an armchair. 'I have just met the man I am going to marry,' she said dreamily.

Michael looked at his sister in disgust and rolled his eyes a Bea. 'That is all she thinks about. I'm off,' he said, heading for the door.

Violet sat up, 'No, wait. I want…' The door closed with a snap before she could finish.

The door opened again immediately and Jane came slowly into the room, just in time to hear Violet say, 'His name is Lord Ridgeworth.'

Bea racked her brains, trying to remember if her landlord had ever been mentioned by name. One look at Jane's face told her it had.

'I have never met a Viscount, apart from Michael, of course.' Bea remarked in what she hoped was an interested voice. 'Is your viscount just as nice?'

Too late Bea remembered that Violet had not actually mentioned Ridgeworth's rank. Fortunately, Violet was too wrapped up in herself to notice.

'He is divine. A bit old but I can put up with that.'

'We did not actually meet Lord Ridgeworth,' Jane said cautiously. 'It was just a chance encounter on Lady Weston's doorstep.'

'He did smile and me and hold my hand,' Violet protested. 'I wish I had not been so untidy.'

'Go to bed, Violet. You have had too much sun your nose is quite pink.'

That was enough to make Violet leap up to look in the mirror. 'Parker must find something to stop it turning into a tan.' With that Violet dashed from the room.

Jane sank into an armchair and sighed. 'I do not know which is more exhausting, Violet in a temper or off in a daydream.' She looked at Bea and shook her head. 'But you will understand why she was so smitten with Ridgeworth. He is incredibly handsome.'

'I never met him. I only know he wanted us all out of the shops at short notice.'

'He is most unlikely to call here. He was polite but nothing more.' Jane changed the subject and asked, 'Did you have a good day with Lily? She can be as tiring as Violet but she always leaves me smiling.'

Bea hesitated, unsure whether to mention seeing Mrs Blakesby. She decided against it. The day after tomorrow she would be on her way back to obscurity. 'We went for a walk, played the piano and some indoor games.' Bea smiled, 'I had to be so careful in answer to all her questions. I am so sorry I cannot stay longer.'

'No. I shall miss you too. I do not think there is much chance of you meeting someone you know but I understand your caution.'

As they climbed the stairs together, they paused to say goodnight to Mrs Hasting's portrait. 'I am sorry you did not get to meet your grandmother,' Jane said softly as Bea lifted a hand to touch the smiling boy. 'She loved John and missed him so much.'

Bea could not reply. There were so many regrets, so many evasions and unanswered questions. It was like a house of cards that could tumbling down at any moment.

Bea spent a restless night. Not actually dreaming but haunted by snippets of memory. The last few days had been full of new sights, experiences and information with no time between to digest what she had learned. The thought that had she would have years to ponder was not as comforting as she would have liked.

It was very early on Sunday morning when Bea finally decided she had tossed and turned enough and got out of bed. Opening the curtains, she could see the sun was shining and the quiet garden called her. Fresh air would blow away the scattered impressions of the night and fortify her for the day ahead.

A splash of cold water on her face would have to do for now. She was not used to being waited upon and did not want to disturb the servants. Her work dresses were easy to fasten and she put on some sturdy shoes. Her hair was still in its night-time braid, a bit straggly but she did not expect anyone to see her.

Bea crept down the stairs intending to access the garden through the morning room window but the door was slightly ajar and she could see a maid sweeping the carpet. Bea knew that if she was seen the maid would instantly offer tea or some other service and more than anything else, she wanted peace and quiet. In the few seconds that she waited for the maid to move out of sight, Bea remembered that the library windows also gave access to the terrace. As silently as she could, Bea scooted across the hall and into the library.

The light was muted here but there was enough to reveal Michael sprawled in an armchair fast asleep. He was still wearing his evening clothes with his cravat removed and the top button of his shirt undone. A half-finished cup of black coffee indicated that the night porter had made an effort to sober him up. Bea hoped the coffee had not been too hot as Michael had missed the saucer and placed the cup directly onto the table's polished surface.

Bea was about to back away when Michael gave a grunt and shifted into a more comfortable position but he did not open his eyes. As quietly as she could, Bea crossed the room and ducked behind the curtains. Behind her Michael snored and Bea hoped it would cover the sound of her sliding up the window sash. Hitching up her skirt she stepped over the low sill and onto the gravel path.

She decided not to close the window in case she could not open it again from the outside.

Bea stepped off the gravel and onto the narrow strip of grass that edged the flower beds and took a deep breath. From her time out here with Lily Bea knew there was a seat just around the corner of the house where she would get the full benefit of the sun and headed that way.

Bea did not know how long she sat there but a tummy rumble reminded her she had not eaten much dinner the night before and it wanted breakfast. She had just reached the window when she heard voices from inside the room. It sounded like Violet and Michael having an argument. She did not want to eavesdrop but if she moved, they might hear the scrunch of gravel and come to see who was lurking in the garden. The curtains muffled the words but Bea heard enough to know they were talking about Lord Ridgeworth. Violet gave a long, mournful groan and there were sounds of movement. Michael's voice was louder and very annoyed. 'Yes, I am sure! One of the younger boys at school was his heir and had to get leave to attend the wedding. And you should not be walking around the house in your nightgown!' More footsteps and the sharp click of the door closing.

Bea did not know if they had both left the room but she could not stay out here all morning. She stepped over the sill and peeped through a gap in the curtains. Michael's chair was empty but Violet was huddled on the sofa crying. Bea closed the window with enough noise to alert Violet and pushed through the curtains. She gave what she hoped sounded like a surprised exclamation. 'Oh! Sorry, I did not know you were there. I have been walking in the garden.'

Violet looked up briefly before covering her face with her hands. Bea risked a step forward. 'I thought you would still be in bed. Is there something wrong?' It was a silly question given that the girl was crying and she did not appear to have been out of bed for very long. Her hair was a tangled golden cloud and she was wearing a loose, ruffled nightgown.

What to do now? As she had not been instantly rebuffed, Bea moved a little closer. 'That was a silly question when you are crying,' she said softly.

'You would cry if your heart was bro-ken.' The last word was split by a hiccup.

Bea almost laughed at Violet being a tragedy queen. 'Nothing can be that bad,' she said bracingly. 'Would you like to talk about it?'

Distress made Violet forget her animosity in favour of having a sympathetic audience. 'I was relying on Michael to arrange for me to meet Lord Ridgeworth properly.'

'Did he refuse?'

'It is worse than that. He is already married!' Violet wailed and buried her face in a cushion. Bea reached out and touched the girl's hand. It was not pushed away so she gently drew Violet up until she could see her face.

'Did you really want to marry an old man?

Violet sniffed and Bea reached into her pocket for a handkerchief and handed it to her cousin. 'It is only the start of the Season. You have plenty of time to find someone better.'

'I don't have time,' Violet insisted. 'I need to be married before anyone hears about the baby.'

Bea's eyes instinctively dropped to the girl's abdomen.

Violet went rigid. 'It is not mine!' She slumped again. 'It's Rose's. Oh, how could she!'

Several things clicked together in Bea's mind. The general unease when Rose was mentioned. Lily's artless comment about not being a bridesmaid. Above all was the thought that Jane had been incredibly brave, or foolish, to invite another potential scandal into her home. The only thing that came out of Bea's mouth was a long-drawn-out and understanding, 'Oh.' Several seconds passed before she added, 'I am so sorry.'

'Not as sorry as I am,' Violet snapped. 'We will be talked about and I will be left on the shelf.'

Bea was getting tired of Violet's self-centred melodrama. But she could not just walk away without trying to help. 'I am sure you won't. You are so pretty the right man will not blame you for your sister's, um, hasty marriage.'

'You don't understand! I fell in love as soon as I saw him. There can never be anyone else.'

It struck a chord and Bea threw caution to the winds. 'I fell in love with an older man when I was even younger than you are.'

'And then married someone terrible!' Violet threw back.

It hadn't been like that but Bea grasped a way of retreating. 'Then don't make the same mistake I did. Why don't you go and talk to your mother?'

'She has gone to church.'

'Then how about some breakfast. Nothing looks quite so bad after tea and toast.'

Violet wiped her eyes. 'Why are you being so nice to me?' It was not quite an admission of her own behaviour but it was a step in the right direction.

'You are family,' Bea said casually. 'I never had one before. Now go and put on one of your lovely dresses, do your hair and smile. I will be green with envy.'

It was not funny but they both laughed. Bea stood up and pulled Violet to her feet. 'I'll peep round the door to see if anyone is about.' Suiting action to words, Bea opened the door a crack and then waved Violet through as though it was part of a game. Violet dashed for the stairs.

Bea followed more slowly. She hoped Violet was not really in love. It was clearly a hopeless situation. Violet thrived on attention and Bea hoped she would not throw herself at the first man who soothed her pride.

'What will everyone think,' Dora muttered as soon as Bea walked into the room. 'I will get another snide comment from madame Parker and a disappointed look from Mrs Duncan. It reflects on me if you walk around improperly dressed and with your hair down.'

Dora's attitude annoyed Bea. Her old friend was not shy of giving her opinion on important matters but her new position as lady's maid was turning her into a petty tyrant. 'Don't worry. Tomorrow we will leave and you can go back to being…' Bea stopped and frowned. Dora had been a friend and mentor but still basically a housekeeper. 'Dora, you don't have to come with me. Mrs Hastings will help you find another position if you really want to be a lady's maid.'

Dora stared at her, open mouthed. 'Not come with you? Of course, I'm coming with you.' She suddenly grinned. 'What would you do without me.'

What indeed! Bea thought as she allowed Dora to fuss over her.

Daisy brought up the breakfast and Bea asked if Mrs Hastings had returned from church.

'No, miss. She usually stays on to teach the Sunday school. Miss Lily has gone with her.'

That left Bea with little to do. Her trunks were nearly packed. Only the best of her gowns was left out for dinner time and her night clothes and toiletries. Reading had always been her choice when there were no chores to do but now that she had ample free time she could not settle with a book. Apart from the wrench of leaving Jane and Lily she would be glad to get away. Settling into her new home would keep her busy for a long time.

A long time sounded bleak and monotonous.

Stop feeling sorry for yourself! You have health and strength and financial security. You have Dora and Freddie!

Bea stood abruptly. It was bad enough being lectured by Dora. She did not need her conscience chiming in. With a determined nod to her reflection in the mirror, Bea marched down the stairs. Another walk around the garden would get her through to lunch time. And she would ask to be shown a door instead of climbing through windows!

Jane joined her in the garden a little later, still wearing her hat and looking worried. 'Bea! Lily told me you were unwell yesterday. Was she too much for you?'

'No, no. We enjoyed a walk. I hope you did not mind me taking her out.'

'Not at all. Going out with Miss Morrison is all the exercise she gets lately.' Jane laughed. 'Not that I am comparing you to a governess.'

Bea chuckled. 'That was what I looked like yesterday. I wore my blacks and became overheated. It real was quite hot in the sun.'

'I found it quite trying,' Jane replied. 'The warmth also brought out the wasps who wanted to share our picnic!'

Sharing meals reminded them both that it was time for lunch. 'I expect Violet is still in bed. She certainly had too much sun yesterday! I just hope she gets over this silly infatuation soon.'

Violet was over it already. She breezed into the morning room in a delightful creation of blue muslin and twirled around. 'What do you think of my gown?'

'I am green with envy,' Bea said with a straight face. Then spoilt the effect by joining Violet's laughter. Jane and Lily looked at them as though they were both mad. But it was a happy madness and Jane managed to forestall her younger daughter's questions. They spent the afternoon quietly in the garden with Violet careful to keep her parasol shading her face. Bea drifted off to sleep for a while and woke up to find herself alone. But not for long.

Lily returned first, followed by maids carrying a jug of lemonade as well as the usual tea things. 'Mama thought you might like lemonade instead of tea. I would have lemonade even on a cold day.'

Jane joined them in time to hear Lily's last words. 'I had to be quite firm to get it. You would think cook had paid for the precious lemons!' Jane poured her tea and defiantly added two slices of lemon and a lump of sugar. 'The one thing I thank the old Viscount for is his hot-houses. They keep us supplied with fruit for most of the year.'

When Lily wandered off to the end of the garden to scatter crumbs for the birds, Bea apologised for falling asleep. 'You must think me very rude.'

'Not at all. I have just been talking to Violet and have to thank you. She really did not deserve your kindness after the way she has been acting.'

Bea brushed it aside. 'Is she feeling better now?'

'Yes, thank goodness. And I had a word with Michael when I got back from church.' Jane grinned 'He is, or was, suffering from his excesses! He has promised to join us for dinner.'

'Your last dinner,' Lily said mournfully. She had lost interest in trying to get the birds to eat from her hands. 'Do you really have to leave so soon?'

The talk turned to Bea's journey the next day. Michael had advised her to go by train and even offered his escort. Jane had understood Bea's fear of meeting someone she knew and insisted Bea use the family coach instead. With an early start the journey could be made in one day.

With that in mind dinner was served earlier than usual. It had highs and lows. Everyone was in harmony and absorbed Bea into the happy family they had always been. But all were to some degree depressed at Bea's leaving.

Saying goodbye next morning was difficult for everyone. Even members of staff came out to wave goodbye. Bea had earned their respect and affection with her natural good manners. Dora had been wary of getting too involved with the staff and they were slightly in awe of her. Freddie on the other hand had thrown himself into the role of footman and had been allowed to keep the black trousers and striped waistcoat in the Lessing colours Mr Samson had found for him.

Hugs and kisses, handshakes and waves were finally over and Bea sat back in her seat as the carriage moved away.

'Here we go again,' Dora remarked wriggling into the deeply cushioned seat. 'More comfortable than that hired carriage.' Within minutes she sank into a contented doze.

Left with only her thoughts for company, Bea tried to raise some enthusiasm for the future. She remembered her Papa saying that life was not always easy. The joys were to be cherished and the woes borne with courage. Recent days had shown Bea how right he was but, in the end, he could not live without his beloved wife.

Bea owed it too herself not to give in to depression. She would build a new life and she would be happy.

Chapter 9

Cambridge. December 1866.

Simon Armitage, Viscount Ridgeworth gazed through the rain spotted window of his carriage as it rolled slowly through the streets of Cambridge. The familiar scenery raised memories that softened his lips but did little else to brighten his sombre expression.

He was an astonishingly handsome man in his prime. His golden hair, blue eyes and perfect features drew admiring glances wherever he went. They had been an asset in his student days. With his wealthy companions he had sampled all the delights the city had to offer. They had played, raced and enjoyed liaisons with willing females. Doing sufficient study to avoid outright failure had been a chore he regretted in later life.

He had not visited the city for many years. At first, he had been enjoying the life of a man about town. But undiluted pleasure had become boring by the time he reached thirty. His parents were urging him to marry, to settle down and raise a family but he was not ready to give up all the pleasures of a man about town.

Things changed when his father's health began to fail. At first, he just seemed lethargic and forgetful but he gradually got worse and Simon had to start taking an interest in his future responsibilities. He found he was woefully unprepared and returned to Cambridge, not as a regular student, to try to catch up on the lessons he had missed. Private tuition and lack of entertainment soon redressed the balance just in time to take over the estates before they fell into trouble.

Somehow that period of intense study had changed his attitudes and way of life. He spent less time in town and more travelling between the Ridgeworths' various holdings, seeing the way lower class people had to struggle to survive and how the law favoured those who already had so much. There was little he could do to change things beyond helping their own tenants and workers but Simon resolved that, when he assumed the title, he would use his powers for the betterment of all.

Simon was in this unsettled state when his mother arrived in town to renew her efforts in finding him a wife. 'The matter is becoming urgent,' she had insisted. 'Your father is beyond useless. He gets lost in his own house and does not know who I am.' Simon understood that she found this distressing as she had a very rigid code of conduct and a husband who wandered around half undressed and accusing the servants of being interlopers was embarrassing. Why this should make his getting married urgent was not clearly explained.

In an effort to give her something else to think about Simon agreed to attend Society events with her and was introduced to Monica Prentiss, daughter of one of his mother's friends. They were thrust into each other's company and Simon was swept him off his feet. Monica had seemed an ideal life-partner, beautiful, charming and admiring of his ambitions. A hasty marriage followed before he had time to think rationally.

On their wedding night Monica had revealed her true character. She had boldly told him she was carrying another man's child. Proving the child was not his would have been impossible. She had cleverly ensured that they had spent long periods alone and were found in a compromising situation.

To protect his family from scandal he had accepted the humiliation of his wife's scorn and spent as little time as possible in her company. Monica had delighted in spending his money, publicly accusing him of neglect and embarking on a series of affairs as soon as the child was born. It was a girl so could have no claim on the title but he had warned her that he would deny any future children.

The disaster of his marriage had shaken Simon to the core, leaving him frozen inside and determined to protect his heart from further damage. He ignored the gossip and immersed himself in work, both for his estate and for the public good.

The increasing rain obscured Simon's view and turned his thoughts to his reason for coming to Cambridge now.

The properties he was to visit were part of Monica's dowry and he could not wait to be rid of them. He had a prospective buyer who had offered a premium for vacant possession. The tenants had been offered generous compensation and help to find other premises. He was here to check that his orders were carried out before the sale was completed.

The carriage drew to a halt in St Anne's Row. A small man Simon assumed was his agent, Tanner, was sheltering in a shop doorway. He rushed forward as soon as the carriage door was opened. 'Lord Ridgeworth, it is an honour to meet you at last.'

Simon took the man in instant dislike. Tanner's servile greeting also carried an insolent note of censure. Simon did not need reminding that he had been negligent in not visiting the properties before. Something else jarred. Tanner seemed far too nervous when he urged Simon to stay in the carriage.

Simon got down and surveyed the row of shuttered shops. They appeared to be in good repair which did not really matter as they were about to be demolished. But it went against his nature to hand over damaged goods. He frowned when he noticed that one, a butcher's, was still open for business.

'I gave him a short extension, so he would not miss out on his Christmas trade,' Tanner panted as he tried to match Simon's swift stride down the road. 'He will be gone before the new year.'

'I will speak to the tenant.'

Simon's suspicions strengthened when Tanner added, 'Please don't trouble yourself, my lord. He is a surly fellow, disgruntled at being told to leave.'

That did not fit with the boon of being granted an extension. More determined than ever to find out what had been going on, Simon ignored the agent and approached the shop. Making a note of the name above the door, he entered the premises.

Two women customers stepped aside to allow him to reach the counter, where he was met by a smiling young man in a striped apron.

Tanner shifted from foot to foot as Simon introduced himself. 'Mr Brown, I am Ridgeworth.'

The butcher showed no surprise. He had taken in Simon's smart appearance and air of command and recognised the name. 'What can I do for you, my Lord. I don't get many gentleman customers.'

Simon glanced at the two women who had their heads together whispering.

'Please serve these ladies then we will talk about your complaint.' Simon stepped back and the women gave him simpering smiles tinged with a little disappointment that they would not be able to hear about Mr Brown's complaint.

The small transactions allowed Simon time to look around. The side bench was well stocked and several fowls hung from hooks. Gleaming knives filled a rack on the wall and the floor was spread with fresh sawdust. The air was fragrant from bunches of dried herbs handing from the ceiling. The butcher treated his customers in an easy manner, even asking after someone called Will. Simon nodded to them as they left the shop and saw Tanner watching through the glass window. He would deal with him later.

Simon waited until the door closed before turning back to the butcher. 'I hear you are unhappy about moving.'

'I won't deny it, my Lord. My father opened the shop more than twenty years' ago. He trained me and I took over when he wanted to retire.'

A woman emerged from the rear of the shop with a baby in her arms and a toddler clinging to her skirt. The glare she directed at Tanner made him scuttle away from the window.

'It's a crying shame, turning us all out and knocking down the shops. We have been good tenants.' The butcher took her arm and tried to guide her into the back room but Mrs Brown still had more to say. 'We did a good trade and had satisfied regulars but the new shop is too far away. We will have to start afresh. 'She started to cry. 'We have a growing family to support like the rest.' She waved a hand as though to include the whole road. 'Except Mrs Fleming and heaven knows what will happen to the dear girl.'

'Please do not distress yourself Mrs Brown.' Simon looked over his shoulder to beckon to Tanner but the man had disappeared, his place taken by a cluster of curious women. The embarrassed butcher was trying to comfort his wife.

'Is there somewhere we could discuss this in private,' Simon asked. 'You have customers waiting but I sense things have not gone well.'

Mr Brown raised his voice, 'Joe, leave what you are doing and mind the shop.'

A boy of about nine or ten came through from the back room. He looked at his weeping mother and frowned at Simon. 'What's up, Pa?' he asked anxiously.

'Never you mind. See to the ladies and take care if you use the knives.' The butcher lifted a flap in the counter and ushered Simon through to the back room and then through another door and up the stairs into cosy kitchen.

Simon spent an interesting half hour. Mr and Mrs Brown answered his quiet questions and volunteered other information. It soon became clear that Tanner had been lining his own pockets. The rent book did not agree with the figures Simon had received from his agent. They had been offered some compensation but less than they were due. They had even paid Tanner a tidy sum to be allowed to stay until after Christmas.

Simon said he was sincerely sorry for the way they had been treated.

'I cannot change the past but be assured Tanner will be punished. If you will furnish me with your new address and the whereabouts of the other tenants, I will see you are amply compensated.

'Thank you,' Mrs Brown said. 'Will you have a glass of ale while Sam gets the other addresses?' Simon accepted and the butcher went down downstairs to the room he used as an office. The ale and a generous slice of veal pie had been consumed by the time he came back.

Mr Brown handed Simon the list, written on the back of an invoice. 'That's most of them. I don't know where Mrs Fleming went.' Simon scanned the neatly written list. Against one of the addresses he was not sure of Mr Brown had added the name of a married daughter who lived in Cambridge.

'Mrs Fleming said she was going to the seaside until she decided where to settle,' Mr Brown added with a frown. 'Poor young lady, turned out with next to no notice on top of being recently widowed.'

Simon did not recognise the name which was hardly surprising. As far as he could remember he had only visited the bookshop once. He looked at the list again and frowned. 'What happened to Mr Hastings who ran the book shop?'

'He died. Miss Hastings took it over with her husband.' Mrs Brown shook her head sadly. 'Then he died too, just before we received notice.' This was worse than anything Simon had imagined.

He felt a stab of guilt for neglecting the properties. None of his tenants had been treated fairly but a woman alone? Simon supressed a shudder. Many of his current activities had to do with working class conditions. He knew the dangers facing unprotected women.

A call from the boy left in charge of the shop broke up the meeting. Simon stood up and said, 'I have kept you from your business for too long. I will set things in train and you will be compensated as you deserve.'

Husband and wife ushered him down the stairs, their thanks overriding each other until Simon could not decipher the words. The shop was crowded. Simon suspected the people were in search of meat for gossip rather than the pot!

It was still raining and Tanner was nowhere in sight. 'Did you see where the agent went?' Simon called up to his driver. The man pointed down the road. 'That way my lord, like a rabbit with a ferret on it tail but I lost sight of him among all the umbrellas.'

'It won't be a ferret,' Simon muttered as he climbed into the carriage. He brushed the worst of the raindrops from his shoulders. It was harder to dislodge the sense of unease.

A remarkably clear image of Miss Hastings filled his mind. Remarkable because he had only met her once when she was little more than a child. It must be because she had seemed mature beyond her years. They had spoken for a few minutes while her father went to find a particular book from the storeroom. He had asked what she was reading in the newspaper spread on the counter and had received a lecture on the iniquities of transportation.

'It is not right', she had declared. 'Not right to be condemned without a chance to defend himself and sent far away from all he knows and loves. How would you feel if your family was starving?'

At first, he had been amused by her passion but her words had stuck. It was not right and his recent work was in trying to improve matters.

Something would have to be done to find her but he had no time to worry about it now as he was already late for his appointment with his buyer.

It was quite late when Simon returned to his hotel room. The deal had been signed but it had irked him to open the meeting with an apology for lateness. In consequence he could not refuse the buyer's invitation to dinner. It had been a long meal with more drinks than Simon was accustomed to. The buyer was a go-ahead businessman from Birmingham who talked incessantly about his growing chain of luxury stores. By the time he escaped Simon's head was reeling.

Noakes, Simon's valet, was a man of few words. He took Simon's hat and coat, asked if his lordship would like some coffee and left the room. When he returned Simon was at a small table writing.

'I have to get this all down while it is still fresh in my mind', Simon said vaguely as Noakes placed the coffee within reach. 'I have been very remiss. I have allowed other people to suffer from my aversions.'

Noakes did not reply. Lord Ridgeworth often used him as a sounding board when he had something on his mind. Ridgeworth took a swallow of coffee and said, 'Sit down.' Noakes did so, at a discreet distance.

'What do you remember of Hastings the bookseller?'

'The one in St Anne's Row?' At Ridgeworth's nod, Noakes thought for a moment. 'A very scholarly man but I suspect he had no head for business When you sent me to him, he was able to select volumes on the subject requested and gave me several for you to choose from. It was his wife who verified my identity and made a note of the titles.'

'Did you ever meet his daughter?'

Noakes actually chuckled. 'Miss Beatrice. Everyone called her Bea because she was always busy.'

'Bea,' Ridgeworth said as though he had suddenly found a gold sovereign. He looked at his silent valet and prompted, 'And?'

Noakes raised an eyebrow. They had been together for many years and Noakes had licence to speak freely. A privilege he seldom used. 'You only asked if I ever met Miss Hastings.'

Simon's coffee grew cold as he told Noakes of the St Anne's Row goings on. 'I have been very selfish. As a result, honest traders have been abused and a gently bred young lady cast adrift.'

'You will find her.' Noakes spoke with confidence. His long service was not due to a handsome salary. He had shepherded a youth through his wild days at university and seen him grow into a conscientious and respected adult. He probably knew more about Simon Armitage than even his closest friends. That knowledge was protected like the crown jewels.

Noakes took away the cold coffee and wished his master goodnight.

Simon made a copy of Mr Brown's list and enclosed it in a letter to his secretary in London along with instructions to pass another copy to his solicitor. Then he went to bed.

Sleep was a long time in coming. He lay awake trying to understand why he was so worried about Miss Hastings, or rather Mrs Fleming. He argued that he would be concerned for any lady cast adrift in a cruel world. But it was more than that. The Hastings had been a cut above the general mode of shopkeepers. They had the stamp of breeding that could not be disguised.

Did she have other relatives? Friends? Members of her husband's family she could turn to? He would not rest until knew she was safe.

Simon slept. And dreamed of Bea. Not a child but a woman he had held in his arms. He could feel the touch of her soft cheek against his.

Next morning Simon walked to the police station to lay a charge against Tanner. He had told Noakes he needed the exercise but it was only an excuse. The dream did not fade as dreams usually did. In fact, his waking mind was adding other details. It was a true memory. He had been in a crowded market when someone knocked her into his arms. Instinctively he had held her until she regained her balance and, in the process, their cheeks had touched. She had looked up at him – then she was gone, swept away by the crowd. He had not thought of the incident since.

Mysteries annoyed him. He dealt in facts. He would find her, ensure her safety and that would be the end of the matter.

The police sergeant listened to Simon's complaint against Tanner and shook his head. 'We can find his address, my lord, but he will be gone by now.'

'I will meet any extra costs in finding him. I am at fault for trusting him and I want justice for the people he has abused.'

Satisfied that he had done all he could for now, Simon returned to the hotel. Noakes had everything packed and ordered the carriage to be brought round.

Simon had prearranged to visit a friend after getting rid of the Cambridge properties and looked forward to a few days of uncomplicated male camaraderie.

Chapter 10

Simon left Cambridge in a lighter mood than he had arrived. Lighter but not completely at ease. The journey to his friend's property near Ipswich was about fifty miles and took the rest of the day, giving Simon far too much time to think about his dream. If he had not recognised Bea at the time, why did he keep thinking of holding her and the softness of her cheek against his?

There was little he could do to distract his thoughts. The persistent rain made it too dark to read and try as he might, he was unable to sleep. It was a relief to finally reach his destination.

It was evening by the time Simon arrived but his friend came out to meet him. Simon leapt from the carriage, threw his arms in the air and shouted, 'All Hail! It was an old joke from school days when Alan had arrived with a trunk marked, A.L.Hayle. Alan had never lived it down. Now, he punched Simon lightly on the shoulder and said, 'Don't you dare do that in front of the children.'

Alan Hayle, Marquis of Truro, was a year or so younger than Simon, a widower with two young children. Unlike Simon his had been a love match. Long sojourns at his ancestral home in Cornwall gave him too much time to think about what might have been so he had purchased a small stud in Suffolk and tried to build a new life.

'How are they?' Simon asked as they went inside. 'In bed, so you have time to recover from your journey.'

After dinner they settled in front of the drawing room fire with a decanter of brandy on the table between them and caught up on recent news. Simon told his friend about the situation he had found in Cambridge. 'I blame myself. I allowed my personal feelings to stand in the way of caring for those properties and the tenants.' He spoke of laying charges against Tanner and ensuring the tenants received compensation. For some reason he did not mention Mrs Fleming.

Alan sipped his brandy and casual remarked, 'I am thinking of marrying again.'

Simon stared in surprise. Alan had, and Simon suspected, still, mourned his wife. 'Do you have anyone in mind?'

'No, but the children need a mother. Why else do widowers remarry?'

'I am being badgered by my mother to think of the title but you already have a son to inherit.'

Simon thought of his own supposed daughter. She was another responsibility he had neglected to check on. But, overall, he considered the child was better off without Monica for a mother.

Alan had moved on to the topic of his stables and a promising colt he was training. The conversation moved easily from horses to current affairs to the weather until it was time to go to bed.

Next morning Simon was woken by a seven-year-old boy jumping on his bed and a smaller girl trying to haul herself up by pulling on the covers. Conscious of his nakedness beneath the sheets, Simon hung on and promised to have breakfast with them if they went back to their nanny straight away.

Alan had made breakfast with his children a priority since the death of their mother. Four-year-old Sarah was too young to have any clear memories but Lionel had been traumatised by the fear his father would leave him too. Alan also saw them into bed at night, which was more than most children could expect. Simon had loved and respected his own father but could not remember him ever coming to say goodnight.

It was too wet and cold for the rest of that day and the next to think of going outdoors for pleasure so the men spent more time with the children. They did trudge out to the stables for an hour or so to school the young animals and examine the mares in foal but the rest of the time was spent playing billiards or cards.

On the third morning the weather changed. It was still cold but the sun was shining and Alan had a sudden whim to take a couple of boats out on the river that formed one of his boundaries. They had both rowed at university and some exercise was welcome.

Simon had not rowed for years and was easily beaten. They were enjoying themselves so much they went further than was wise and returned tired and aching. They just had time for a quick bath and change of clothes before saying goodnight to the children. After a leisurely dinner they were both ready for an early night.

Sore muscles and the smell of the liniment Noakes had applied with a liberal hand gave Simon a restless night. Towards dawn he dreamed of Bea again.

Bea threw herself into his arms. As he held her close, the brim of his hat dislodged her bonnet and their cheeks touched. She looked at him with wide, hazel eyes and opened her mouth to speak but was swept away by the milling crowd. The sense of loss was so intense that Simon cried out.

For the first time in years Simon awoke with an erection. As dreams do, the sensation was fading, along with his arousal.

He lay there for a moment, stunned.

Monica's betrayal had emasculated him as surely as if she had wielded a knife. Determined not to allow her the triumph of seeing him beaten, he had flirted and danced with any lady who made overtures. But there was never any desire to take things further. He ended the liaisons before they became too intense with the excuse of honouring his marriage vows. Most of the ladies accepted rejection with a romantic sigh. Most of the men thought him a fool for not taking what was offered.

As he became fully awake, he wondered why the dream was so closely matched to the memory of that chance encounter. It had only lasted for a second or two and been quickly forgotten.

Simon got up impatiently and rang for his valet. He would return to London and set a reliable investigator to find her and reassure him of her safety. Then he could get her out of his mind and dreams.

Or not, a small voice prodded. *Whether you like it or not she means something to you.* 'Nonsense,' he said aloud, startling Noakes.

'You spoke, my lord?'

Simon pulled himself together. 'Yes. I have decided to return to London. You may start packing as soon as I am dressed.'

Alan took the news of Simon's sudden departure with a raised eyebrow. 'You are tired of our company already, old chap. Or have the children been too much for you?'

'I have remembered something that must be done before the Christmas holiday. I need to prepare a speech for the House and did not bring my notes.'

It was a lame excuse but Alan accepted it without further comment. The children cried when he said goodbye which made him feel guilty.

Simon decided to take the train to London. His carriage and most of his luggage would carry on to Gloucestershire where he had planned to spent Christmas.

There was no direct rail link to London so Simon had to suffer the added frustration of changing trains and kicking his heels on a draughty platform while he waited for the connection. Now he had decided to get the matter sorted he wanted it done as soon as possible.

He had forgotten to post the letter to his secretary which made him even more testy. He was usually well organised. He did not forget things.

Certainly not Miss Hastings!

'Oh, shut up!' He snarled making a passing couple turn around and glare at him. Simon turned away. He was not going to tell complete strangers he was talking to himself.

Noakes was standing too far away to hear what had been said but Ridgeworth had clearly insulted the men who had crossed his path. Something was very wrong to make his usually polite master so unsettled.

Thank goodness for swift transport and telegrams, Simon thought when they eventually reached London. Most of his staff had been given leave over Christmas and would not be expecting him back until the New Year. But his carriage was waiting and he was soon at his own home.

Simon hurried inside and handed his coat and hat to the butler. 'Good evening, Stepping. Have some light refreshment sent to my study and alert Mr Peters.'

'Mr Peters is already there, my lord. He is checking that everything is ready for your attention.'

There could not be much of note, Simon thought as he walked through the house. Parliament was in recess and most of his friends would already have gone to their homes for the holiday. But Peters was quite young and eager to impress with his efficiency. Simon frowned. Or was it that Peters had nowhere to go? He gave a huff of annoyance. Now he was worrying about how his staff spent their free time!

Peters sat quietly while his employer ate sandwiches, drank coffee and leafed through his mail. Simon pushed the papers and tray aside. 'There is nothing that cannot wait. I have a more taxing task for you.' He drew out the letter he had forgotten to post. 'Most of is in there. It was quicker to bring it as I have other business to attend to tomorrow. I will add to the solicitor's letter as follows.' Simon gave Peter's his notes on Tanner and continued. 'Please liaise with the Cambridge police. I may need to give evidence in person.' Peters wrote everything down and waited for his next instruction. 'Make extra copies of this list of names, one each for the bank and one to go with my letter to Mr Lawrence authorising the extra payments. I will have the original back when you are done.' Peters gathered up the papers. 'I will see to it straight away.'

'Not tonight. I will be going out in the morning on other business so you may do it then.'

Simon dismissed his secretary and waited for Bea to invade his senses. He felt rather disappointed when she did not appear. 'Dratted woman,' he grumbled. 'I am going out of my way to find you and you cannot even say thank you. And now I am talking to myself again.'

He marched from the room and upstairs to change for dinner. A lonely dinner but well prepared at short notice. He missed having someone to talk to while he dined but it need not be a lonely evening. He and Noakes both enjoyed a game of chess. They were evenly matched and, once the pieces were set out, there was no servant and master. Noakes played to win.

It was a long game and Noakes was pleased to his that his lordship had sorted out his problem. His own lapse of concentration lost him the game.

Before he retired Simon told Noakes to lay out the suit he wore when visiting factories and have a hackney at the door by nine the next morning.

Now what was up? Noakes thought as he left the room.

Simon's destination next morning was a respectable looking house near Euston Station. A small brass plaque proclaimed it to be the office of Samuel Jones, Private Investigator. He was admitted by a porter who glanced at his card and showed him into a comfortable waiting room. Lords were not left to cool their heels in the hallway.

Almost immediately two men came through the inner door. The elder was Samuel Jones, ex-Bow Street Runner. He looked like a prosperous business-man in a smart suit who enjoyed his food and comforts but he had not lost his ability to assess people. He greeted Ridgewood in a polite but not subservient manner and invited him into his office. 'This is my son, Abel,' he said waving to the younger man. 'Abel by name and able by his own wits and my training. Take a seat and tell us how we can help you.'

Simon had used Jones' services before and knew him to be both discreet and efficient.

It did not take long to explain his mission. 'The lady is not in any trouble, I hope. I just feel a responsibility for her sudden eviction.'

They discussed how the case would be managed. Jones senior no longer did the leg work and it was the younger man who suggested posing as an agent for one of Mrs Fleming's elderly relations, a great aunt or godmother. 'I will suggest that Mrs Fleming could be in for a nice surprise,' he said, tapping one finger to the side of his nose and winking.

Ridgeworth agreed with a smile. He turned to Jones senior. 'I see you have trained him well. He turned back to the younger man. 'Do not contact Mrs Fleming directly unless she is in dire straits. Just locate her, see that she is comfortably settled and report back to me.'

He rose to his feet, shook hands and placed a bulky envelope on the desk before being shown to the door.

Simon had dismissed his cab but soon found another to take him to Bond Street. He had intended asking Alan what his children would like as Christmas gifts but it had slipped his mind in the rush to leave. Lionel would not be a problem. He was much the same age as one of his nephew's. Surely all boys liked toy soldiers and things that made a noise. What to buy for a four-year-girl was beyond him.

The toy shop assistant was very helpful. She laid out a selection of dolls, colouring materials other bits and pieces. Simon chose a soft-bodied doll with extra clothes that could be taken off and on, a monkey that turned somersaults and some brightly coloured beads. He gave the address for delivery and signed the bill without blinking an eye at the price.

He was almost at the shop door when he noticed a little girl gazing longingly through the shop window. His conscience tweaked and he returned to the counter. 'Have the same girl things sent to this address and add them to the bill. He wrote his mother-in-law's address on the back of one of his cards and left, well satisfied with his morning's work.

Chapter 11

The next day Simon set off for his brother's home in Stroud. A telegram had been sent with the time of his arrival and a carriage was waiting at the station to meet him.

His eldest nephew, John, rushed forward to greet him. 'Uncle Simon! We are so glad you decided to come early.' At thirteen years of age John Armitage closely resembled his father and uncle. He was Simon's heir, after his father and the prospect did not please him. He was more interested in running his maternal grandfather's woollen mill.

Talking all the time, John led the way to the waiting carriage. 'We were surprised when your carriage arrived without you. I thought you might be riding but the coachman said you had to go back to London.'

Simon allowed the lad to rattle on, adding a few words here and there as they travelled the short distance to his brother's home.

Rev James Armitage lived in a rambling vicarage in the centre of Stroud. A steep driveway led to a wide sweep of gravel surrounded by empty flower beds. In summer it would be a blaze of colour as Maria, Mrs Armitage was a keen gardener.

Maria came out to meet him. She was a small, dark-complexioned lady with an increasingly round figure. Her brown hair bore the first streaks of grey but the only lines on her face were from her almost constant smile. Simon just had time to embrace her before he was besieged by two young boys.

Ralph aged eight and six-year-old Peter took after their mother. It was too early to tell but Simon doubted they would ever be more than pleasantly good looking. They made up for their lack of looks with lively natures.

Simon relaxed. This was what he needed. A few weeks in the uncomplicated warmth of a happy family.

'Peter is out visiting a sick parishioner,' Maria told him as they made their way indoors. It was not a grand residence. The furniture was well polished but bore the scars of an active family. It smelled of lavender and freshly baked bread. Maria kicked aside a boot and bent to pick up a discarded jacket that she handed to Ralph with the order to put it on the hall stand where it belonged. It was sometimes even more chaotic but it was a home in every sense of the word.

From the moment their took off their coats, Simon and Noakes were absorbed into the body of the Armitage household. There was no other way to describe it. James Armitage's calling was the skeleton upon which their lives were built. His family were the flesh and love its beating heart.

They all trooped through to the large kitchen where the maid was setting out teacups and plates of food. The family timetable was based on James' parish duties but not dominated by them. If, as now, James was out meals were taken, bed and school times observed. Somehow James would make time to spend with his family. Whenever possible he set aside an hour before the evening meal for family only.

Everyone sat down, including Noakes, the housekeeper and the maid. Maria said grace, an informal thanks for the food and the arrival of Simon and Noakes.

'Amen,' they chorused and the younger boys made a grab for the cakes. 'Visitors first,' Maria told them.

'Uncle's not a visitor. He's family,' Ralph replied, but passed the plate to Simon anyway.

Simon laughed. 'When I was a boy, we had to eat the bread and butter first.'

'Then we might not have room for cake,' Peter said worriedly with one eye on his mother.

Only one other member of the family was missing. 'Where is Iris?' Simon asked.

'James is fetching her from school tomorrow.'

Simon smiled and caught Noakes doing the same. Iris had that effect. She was a tiny, fairy-like creature with the Armitage golden hair and blue eyes but it was her sunny nature that made everyone smile. Simon had not seen her since she started school and was looking forward to hearing how she was enjoying it.

The younger boys attended a local school but John was a weekly boarder at a Grammar School on the other side of town.

'Have you thought any more about going to University?' Simon asked John.

His nephew grimaced. 'It is bad enough being at school all week. I only get to help Grandpa at weekend and holidays.' He was referring to Maria's father who owned a large woollen mill. John had set his heart on running it one day but he was also Simon's heir and needed to be more prepared to take on the role and responsibilities of a Viscount. The matter would need to be discussed but there would be plenty of time in the week ahead.

When tea finished, they dispersed. The children, according to their age, had chores to do. Maria only had a resident housekeeper and maid with a daily woman coming in and also taking away the laundry. It was not for lack of money. James' ethic of service was part of their lives which they accepted as naturally as breathing. Simon was willing to give a hand when needed but did not think it would suit him long term. He thought he treated his servants well with good wages and reasonable free time but he expected his home to run smoothly without being bothered with the details.

Noakes had gone to unpack and Simon took the opportunity to ask Maria what had happened to the gifts he had sent with the carriage. 'They are safely tucked away in James' study.' She wagged a finger at him. 'Too many, as usual.'

'Who else should I spend my money on?' Maria raised an eyebrow but didn't reply and his conscience made Simon add, 'I sent gifts to Cynthia.' Maria merely looked away with a sad shake of her head. She did not know the true facts of Cynthia's parentage and had given up asking Simon when they would get to meet her. 'Too young,' was an excuse getting thinner with each passing year.

Simon liked his sister-in-law. James had met and married her while he was still a curate, much to the disgust of his class-conscious mother. Alliance with trade was taboo and she refused to receive Maria. For her part, Maria was not ashamed of her background although she never made any effort to mix with her husband's aristocratic friends. As far as family went there was only Simon and her mother-in-law. One always warmly welcomed, the other spoken of with respect in front of her children.

James had still not returned when it was time for the evening meal. The younger boys had gone to bed after their supper so only Maria, Simon and John were in the dining room and already eating their soup when James walked in. He looked tired. He said Hello to Simon and told Maria that Mr Brewer had died. 'Give me a few moments. I must go up to say goodnight to the boys.'

Maria delayed the serving of the next course until James re-joined them.

'No soup for me,' James said as he took his place at the table. 'I am awash with the tea Mrs Brewer kept making.'

'I will visit her tomorrow while you go to fetch Iris,' Maria said softly. 'Things will be very hard for her with no family to rally around.'

The conversation turned to other activities planned for the next few weeks. Many were concerned with church and parish duties. Simon was not actually asked to take part but knew he would be drawn in, mainly by the children.

It was late in the evening when Simon and his brother settled in comfortable chairs by the drawing room fire. A decanter stood on a small table between them but they had hardly sipped from the glasses in their hands. They had so much to talk about but Simon did not know where to start.

As though reading his mind James said, 'Do you want to talk about it?'

Simon smiled. James would never utter a demanding, What's wrong? He just opened a door and invited people to walk in.

Simon had always admired his younger brother and they shared a close bond. Talking to James was cathartic, like confessing without being condemned.

'I have sold the Cambridge properties.' Simon had no need to explain his reasons. James was the only person who knew Cynthia was not his true daughter. Even so, he had offered to take the child into his own home when her mother died.

Having started, Simon poured out his feelings. 'Now I feel free to start a new life,' he ended.

'Monica cannot be erased no matter how much you wish it. She is part of who you are. And there is always Cynthia to remind you.'

Simon took a gulp of brandy to wash the bitterness from his mouth and mind. 'I have sent her Christmas gifts.'

'Sent? You did not think to take them yourself?'

The truth stung and Simon offered the first excuse that came into his head. 'I did not have time.'

James raised an eyebrow. 'You arrived here three days earlier than expected.' Simon squirmed under his brother's sorrowful regard. The last time he had seen Cynthia was just after Monica died. She had been a grizzling toddler who bore no likeness to her beautiful mother. Which should have been a bonus but only reminded him that she was fathered by another man.

The silence became uncomfortable. To fill it Simon said, 'I will settle the proceeds of the sale on her. She will have an ample dowry when the time comes.' It was a spur of the moment decision as he had originally intended to use the money to compensate the tenants.

James changed the subject and asked if Simon had enjoyed his visit with Truro. He knew Alan from schooldays although they had never been very close friends.

This was much easier to talk about and he gave a detailed record of their activities. 'I had a great time. We even rowed down the river!' Simon laughed, 'He beat me hollow. He is thinking of marrying again although he has no-one specific in mind at present. He says the children need a mother.'

Simon took a sip of his brandy and turned the subject away from children and marriage.

'I had to cut the visit short to go back to London.' It was actually a relief to talk about Tanner's fraud which brought him to the matter that was really playing on his mind.

'Do you believe it is possible to be haunted by a living person?'

'I am not sure you can be haunted by a dead one.' James eased away from that path, it led back to Simon's obsession with his dead wife. 'Why do you ask?'

Simon finished his brandy and considered topping up his glass but he did not need another kind of spirit addling his mind. His account was disjointed but the only thing he omitted was how graphic one of his dreams had been.

At the end of the recital he waited for his brother's advice. It was slow in coming and couched in impersonal terms.

'The mind is a funny thing. It retains knowledge we are not consciously aware of. A seemingly insignificant event can be stored away until something happens to bring it out for consideration. Imagination them builds a fantasy around it until one does not what to believe.' He returned to the present situation. 'I think you have done the right thing in ensuring Mrs Fleming is safely settled. It should put your mind at ease.' James frowned, deep in thought. 'Do you think she might be connected to the Lessings? Their family name is Hastings and you say the Cambridge Hastings appeared genteel?'

'That is certainly a lead for Jones to follow. The family have only recently come into Society so I don't know very much about them.'

The matter was left there and, shortly after, they went to bed.

Chapter 12

Simon slept well, undisturbed by dreams. He was woken by the sound of an argument beyond his bedroom door.

'You can't go in there!'

'But I want to tell Uncle what you did.'

Noakes' voice came next. 'What are you two imps doing here? No, don't tell me. Get yourselves downstairs. I'll come and play trains with you after breakfast.'

Simon smiled. Noakes was quite at home here. He lost his reserve and had a particular relationship with the younger boys.

Simon was already out of bed when Noakes entered the room. 'Good morning, my Lord. Did the boys disturb you?'

'They were making enough noise to waken the dead.' It was said with a laugh and Noakes was pleased to see that his master had recovered from his recent distracted mood. Ablutions completed the two men went down to breakfast together. It was another informal meal in the kitchen. They were just in time to hear the cause of the boys' argument.

'He poured water in my bed and told Sally I had wet myself.'

'Well, you stole my cake at supper,' Ralph replied. 'I was saving it for bedtime.'

'That is no excuse. You are not allowed food in the bedroom. You were both in the wrong and I do not want to hear another word about it,' Maria was saying as Simon and Noakes entered the kitchen.

Maria had just wished the men good morning when James joined them. The boys looked at their mother apprehensively but she just nodded her head and told them to sit down.

James led the brief morning prayers and looked around to see if anyone had anything to add. 'We have been naughty,' Ralph muttered.

'Again?' James said gravely. Both boys nodded. 'Are you sorry?' 'Yes,' the boys chorused. 'Then we will say grace and have our breakfast.'

Simon silently applauded his brother's tactics. In a few short words he had registered his disappointment and expected remorse. It was far more effective than a demand to know the details and allot punishment. His own father had not been a harsh parent but misdemeanours were dealt with in the formal setting of his study. Followed by a lecture on responsibility and honour. James led by example rather than goading people along with a metaphorical stick.

In the course of the general conversation James mentioned going to collect Iris from school. 'I should like to go with you,' Simon said as the maid took his empty bowl. It was another opportunity to spend precious time with his brother. The informal meal allowed everyone, including the housekeeper and maid, to say what they had planned for the day. The subtle division between their ranks still existed. The servants did not pretend to be family and the boys did not speak over an adult.

'John and I were going to the mill,' Maria said when everyone left the table, but I must call on Mrs Brewer first. John, if you can, please try to persuade your grandfather to take a break over the holiday. I am sure he does not need to work all day and every day.'

'I am working in the carding room today,' John added. He wrinkled his nose. 'I am going to suggest that everyone wears a mask as the fluff makes you cough.' Simon knew a great deal about factory conditions and wished other employers were so caring of their workers.

The distance between Stroud and Gloucester was only eight or so miles as the crow flies. The journey by carriage, along twisty roads and up and down steep hills took nearly two hours.

The conversation of the night before was not mentioned but the brothers had plenty to talk about. 'I hope John manages to persuade Mr Wallace to stay with us for a few days,' James remarked as they passed the mill. He looked at Simon with a twinkle in his eyes. 'Mama will not be joining us.'

Simon laughed aloud. It was no surprise and more of a relief than it ought to have been. 'But you still ask her year after year.'

''I dislike closed doors.' That just about summed up James' philosophy.

'I shall have to visit Mother before I go back to London,' Simon said reluctantly. It would not be a pleasure. Lady

Ridgeworth was a coldnatured women, who had always been rigid in her opinions. Once set they could not be changed by argument or reason. She had been the main promoter of his marriage to Monica and blamed Monica's later behaviour on Simon for his seeming neglect. Admittedly she did not know the child was not his but took no interest in it anyway.

'I had planned to take the children to visit in the New Year.' A slow smile spread across James' lips. 'Would you be willing to take them?'

'Oh, vicar!' Simon mocked, 'I am ashamed of you.' It was untrue and they both knew it. James had endured years of rebukes and still visited his mother regularly. But no-one could force affection. 'It will be a pleasure,' Simon said, referring to the previous question. 'I don't see enough of them.'

'A mixed pleasure,' James remarked wryly., glossing over Simon's reluctance to visit Cynthia. 'By the time you get to Bath you may have changed your mind.'

'We will go by train. That should distract them.'

They moved on to discussing current affairs and Simon's political activities. It lasted until they drew up outside the school.

It was an imposing stone house set high on a hill overlooking the city of Gloucester. They did not waste time admiring the view as it was very cold and James did not want to keep the horses standing for too long.

The front door was opened by the headmistress, Miss Waring. She was a thin, severe looking lady of middle years. She invited them into her office while Iris said goodbye to her friends. James declined her offer of refreshment with the excuse of not keeping the horses standing.   Simon was intrigued by the office furnishings. Half of the room was business like with bookshelves, desk and wall charts. The other end, closer to the fireplace was more like a sitting room. Miss Waring subtly directed the men to a sofa and took the chair opposite. Simon had a feeling the teacher was not pleased by his presence and the seating was deliberate so she could keep him under scrutiny. She made polite but stiff conversation and subjected Simon to a gimlet stare through her wire framed spectacles whenever he spoke. He came to the conclusion that she hated men.

The change in Miss Waring's manner when Iris joined them was starling. She placed an arm across Iris' shoulders and said, 'I was just about to tell your Papa how well you have settled in and made friends.' She actually raised a smile for James. 'It is sometimes difficult for girls to adjust to living in a large group.'

Miss Waring escort them out to the carriage and wished them all a very Happy Christmas.

The coachman had already loaded Iris' luggage and had the door open. Before she climbed inside Iris waved to an upstairs window. Simon followed her glance and saw a pale face surrounded by bright ginger hair pressed against the glass. 'That was Joanna, my best friend,' Iris said as the carriage started to move. 'She has to stay here because her mother is dead and her Papa is in India. She is very clever and she can do hard sums in her head. Even really hard ones if she works them out on a slate.' Iris laughed. 'There are not many of those because Joanna knows more than the teachers.'

Simon thought the girl sounded like a precocious brat.

His brother took a different view. 'Would you like her to bring her home with you for the holidays?'

Iris bounced with excitement. 'Oh, thank you, Papa. Thank you.'

Simon saw the invitation as just another example of his brother's constant need to draw all waifs and strays into the fold. He dismissed the girl from his mind and concentrated on Iris.

She was well worth looking at. At first glance she appeared frail, as though a puff of wind would blow her away. She had the Ridgeworth blonde hair and blue eyes but resembled her mama in her robust character. Even at eleven it was easy to see she would become a great beauty. Iris seemed unaware of her looks, or anyone else's. Her descriptions of friends and teachers all dealt with characteristics. She was obviously fond of Miss Waring but Joanna's name and opinions were quoted frequently.

It seemed a strange friendship and Simon had an uncomfortable memory of Monica. She had surrounded herself with less attractive girls so she could shine but Iris was too artless to behave like that and he hoped she never would be.

They talked about the coming Festival and Iris' enthusiasm was infectious. Simon found himself offering to cut holly and lend his height in the placement of decorations in high places. Iris planned to help Mrs Savage, the housekeeper, to cook mince pies and biscuits for the carol singers and accompany her mother when she delivered baskets of goodies to some of the poorer parishioners.

It was all so different to his own upbringing. Rigid decorum had been the order of the day. His father had been a quietly conscientious parent. He had spent time with his sons, instilling a sense of duty but only showing his affection by praising their efforts and successes and only when they were alone. Simon had a vague memory of his mother complaining that praise made a boy idle and it was easier for all concerned if she was not upset. Simon did not like to think his father had been afraid of his wife but knew they barely tolerated each other. Simon had never seen them genuinely relaxed when they were in the same room, which was as seldom as they could manage. In public they were rigidly polite.

Until his health failed, his father had done all he could to prepare Simon for his future role but he had not been a very good student until it was almost too late. Simon was now determined to prepare John so he did not make the same mistakes.

Simon did not think it likely. John's upbringing would stand him in good stead whichever way life took him. Responsibility was bred into his bones. Simon envied him.

He could not help comparing their backgrounds. It was also in sharp contrast to how he had lived in recent years. After his marriage he had dedicated himself to his responsibilities and keeping up a façade of honourable virtue. In truth it had felt more like isolation. His father's death soon after he married Monica had given him an excuse to spend little time with her and an opportunity to use his new position to take an active part in politics. He was always busy but experienced little true happiness.

Being with Alan and his family, and now with his own, had awoken a desire for the same relaxed and loving way of life. But to do that he would need to marry again. He was not willing to take the risk.

Simon was recalled to the present by a repeated question from Iris. He apologised for wool-gathering and put his uneasy thoughts aside.

The following days were filled with activities. There was holly to cut and tied to stair rails. Bows and tinsel were refurbished and placed on the Christmas tree. Simon and Noakes moved furniture, carried coal buckets and generally made themselves useful.

Simon was not sure he would always want to live quite so democratically but it was fun for a while.

The highlight of his visit was the midnight Nativity service.

Simon had not been to church since Monica's funeral and his feelings on that occasion could not be classed as prayers. His more recent visits to Stroud had been arranged to avoid Sundays as it would have saddened his brother if he had refused to go to church.

This time there was no avoiding the service.

The church was packed for the midnight service. The congregation sang with gusto and Simon found the words learned in childhood were instantly remembered.

James' sermon almost moved Simon to tears. He had a feeling it was directed at him but he could see that other members of the congregation were also taking his words to heart. Love. That was the essence. Love for God being shown in care for others. James' concluding words stuck in his mind. 'Love has no limits. The more you give the more you receive. God's blessing of love be with you all, now and always.'

Every one said, 'Amen.'

It was another cold and clear night and people did not linger to talk. They called out their good wishes and hurried home. Simon carried Peter who had slept through most of the service but no-one had even thought of leaving him at home. Ralph was manfully plodding along, protesting that he was not tired at all and could he start opening his presents. He accepted 'No' with a shrug and followed Simon and his burden up the stairs.

The adults did not stay up for very much longer. James had another service in a few hours' time so they all went to bed.

The rest of Simon's visit passed far too quickly. When all the feasts had been eaten, gifts given and received the household settled back into its normal routine.

Chapter 13

Before New Year Simon took the children to visit their grandmother in Bath. She had moved there even before the death of her husband. Seeing him deteriorate into a bumbling idiot had offended her sense of proper behaviour. She had displayed dutiful grief at his funeral but her sons both knew it was only for show.

The children had accepted the news of the visit with mixed feelings. On the one hand they did not want to go and on the other the prospect of an outing with their uncle promised excitement.

They all enjoyed the novelty of travelling by train. It was not the children's first experience but a rare enough event to make the younger boys very excited. John showed off his superior experience by summoning porters and hackneys and keeping an eye on his younger brothers. Iris was the perfect little lady, accepting with a smile any hand offered to help her in and out of the train and the cab that took them to her grandmother's door. When the cab stopped Peter grabbed Simon's hand and whispered, 'I don't like grandmother.' Simon agreed but, in loco parentis, felt obliged to say, 'That was not polite.'

Lady Ridgeworth received them, it could not really be called a greeting, in a drawing room stuffed to overflowing with furniture and knick-knacks. She sat in a throne-like chair that she needed a footstool to reach and did not show any pleasure in seeing the children.

She was a small woman with a taste for flamboyant clothing. Simon was sure her elaborately styled hair owed is rich colour to dye and her complexion to cosmetics.

'Do not stand in the doorway. I do not like draughts,' Lady Ridgeworth said loudly. They trooped forward and, in the process, Ralph bumped into a small table laden with ornaments. John neatly fielded a glass bowl and put it back on the table.

'Just as clumsy as ever,' Lady Ridgeworth snorted and turned her attention to Peter who was trying to hide behind Simon's legs. 'Come here, boy, and make your bow.' Peter emerged just long enough make a jerky movement with his head and retreated again. 'No manners and far too fat. He doesn't get that from MY side of the family.'

Iris received only a cursory glance as she made a graceful courtesy. The old lady's eyes were rivetted on John and she actually smiled. 'Ah, you are so like your grandfather. Come as sit by my side.' She waved a hand at Iris and the younger boys. 'You know your way upstairs. I will speak to you later.' It sounded like a threat. Simon shepherded the relieved youngsters to the door but was not allowed to escape. 'Not you. As you have taken your time in visiting your mother, you can wait a little longer.'

John was alternately questioned and praised by his grandmother until he mentioned visiting the mill. 'I told your father to put a stop that,' the lady said angrily. 'You should not be mixing with people like that.' She shook her head. 'It is bad enough that you have to endure it at home.'

John stiffened and took a deep breath but did not reply. His grandmother pursed her lips. 'She has ruined you.'

The inference was clear. Simon realised his mother was deliberately goading the boy and intervened. 'John, go and join the others.' John looked quickly at the old lady's contorted face and rushed from the room.

'How dare you,' she spluttered, to enraged to speak clearly. 'I give the orders in this house.'

'I do not wish to quarrel with you, mother, but is it unfair to lead the boy into disparaging his mother.'

'You have changed since you lost your wife. You have never been so rude to me before.' For the first time ever, Simon heard a note of disappointment, almost pain in her voice.

Simon answered the first comment. 'I changed before that. Now I work for people who cannot defend themselves from abuse. And that includes seeing a young boy goaded to the end of his endurance. I am proud of John. Now, if you will excuse me.' Simon took a pace towards the door.

'Don't go.'

Simoon turned. Was his mother pleading? If so, it did not show on her face which was tight lipped as ever. But she suddenly looked every one of her sixty-three years. He softened and went to sit on the chair John had vacated. 'I am sorry if I was rude but you were being cruel. They are lovely, well brought-up children. They could bring brightness into your life if you would let them.'

'I do not know what you are talking about.' The haughtiness had returned and Simon gave up trying to reason with her. He searched for words to bridge the uncomfortable silence.

His mother had no such problem. As though the previous few minutes had been wiped from her mind she said, 'I have been waiting for you to visit. I wish to go to Harrogate for the summer so you must send one of your carriages. One never knows who has been riding in a hired vehicle.'

Simon almost laughed. It was either that scream in frustration. He was saved by the dressing gong. Even living in solitary state Lady Ridgeworth upheld the habits of high society.

Simon went first the top floor. These rooms were sparsely furnished with pieces Lady Ridgeworth had tired of but it seemed cosier than the over-stuffed drawing room. John perched on the window ledge while Iris sat on a bed with a young brother on either side. The book in her hand suggested she had been reading to them. On the table was a tray of plates that reassured him they had been fed. It was not a forgone conclusion. His mother's staff never acted on their own initiative and he could not be sure what orders she had given for their care.

'Are you alright up here,' Simon asked. Iris shrugged, 'It is where we always stay.'

'When Papa brings us, we have nice meals down stairs,' Peter added. The boy was obsessed with food!

John added bitterly, 'I would prefer bread and water up here.'

'Do we have to stay here very long?' Iris asked quietly.

'As least for tonight,' Simon told them. 'Leave it with me.'

It caused quite a stir when Simon entered the kitchen. 'Please send up to the children whatever you have planned for dessert. Milk and biscuits later.'

The cook and maid stared with open mouths when he left the room.

Simon and his mother dined alone. It was very civilised. A uniformed footman accepted trays from a maid at the door and served at table. The maid came back to clear the empty plates.

Simon's were almost licked clean as the portions had been very small.

Then tea was served with equal pomp in the drawing room. Through it all Lady Ridgeworth kept the conversation of platitudes. She waited until the servants left the room before asking, 'Have you made any progress in finding a new wife?'

Simon groaned. His mother had been sending him letters on the subject since the day his year of mourning was up. She must have had it marked on her calendar.

'Not yet.' Then he had to listen to a lecture on securing the succession, his advancing age and regret that Monica had only managed to produce a girl. Simon was too weary for another argument and made noncommittal replies and insincere promises to look at this year's crop of debutantes.

Simon managed to navigate several other controversial subjects and they parted in reasonable amity. Lady Ridgeworth's final order was that he be ready to escort her to the Pump Room at 11am next morning.

He went back to the top floor. In the first room the younger children were all in bed and only Iris was awake. 'Thank you for the puddings,' she whispered. 'I have listened to Ralph and Peter's prayers.' He kissed her forehead and went next door to see John.

The boy lay flat on his back and turned his head towards the door as it opened. Even in the semi-darkness Simon could see the tension in John's face and the rigidity of his body. Simon sat on the edge of the bed. 'Can't you sleep?' he asked softly.

'I never do sleep well here.' John bit his lips as though trying to hold back his words. Simon waited, a tactic he had learned from his brother. After a moment or so John asked, 'Why is grandmother so nasty? Even when she is saying nice things to me, she is also implying…. Oh, I don't know how to put it.' John gave a frustrated huff.

'Don't take it personally. I have been in for my share of the criticism.' Simon paused, choosing his words carefully. 'It can be difficult to explain without speaking ill of my mother. Please just accept that she is a very unhappy person. I am proud of you. You acted like a true gentleman.'

'Now you are going to talk about going to university and my duty to the title,' John groaned.

''Not exactly. But it is something you have to consider.'

John hitched himself higher so he was looking at, rather than up to his uncle. 'Why is it considered honourable to inherit wealth and position simply because of how, or to whom you were born, and despised if you work hard?'

'I don't know. Inheriting a title is also hard work at times. That is why I would like you to go to university. I was woefully unprepared and made mistakes I hope you will avoid.'

'If you married again and had a son…'

'That is most unlikely to happen,' Simon interrupted. 'And if I did have a son, I will be an old man before he reached his majority. He will need you to guide him.'

John sighed and slid back down the bed. 'I will think about it but everyone forgets that I have a duty to Grandpa Wallace too.'

'There is no need to worry about it right now.' He squeezed the boy's shoulder and said goodnight wishing he could have been more comforting.

Next morning Simon told the maid who brought up his hot water that he would eat breakfast upstairs with the children. His mother took hers in her room.

'When can we go home?' Peter asked again.

'Tomorrow. I will take you out this afternoon,' Simon said to cheer them up. He had thought of forcing his mother to spend time with them but decided that least said, soonest mended.

He was waiting in the hall when his mother came down stairs at ten minutes to eleven. Unable to reprimand him for lateness she snapped at the footman to open the door.

Lady Ridgeworth did not keep a carriage of her own. The steep streets of Bath made it impractical and she seldom travelled further afield. She rode in a sedan chair with Simon walking by her side. He actually enjoyed the exercise.

Bath was not as fashionable as it had been a generation ago. Most of the people they met were elderly or infirm. The few younger women he was introduced to were either bold widows or tongue-tied schoolgirls. Simon refused to sample the water and wandered off to speak to an elderly gentleman he barely knew.

Over a meagre lunch he said he was taking the children out for an hour or so. 'We will be back in time to join you for tea.'

'They are not coming down for dinner,' was Lady Ridgeworth's only comment. Simon accepted it as a concession.

Simon and the children enjoyed a look around the shops and freedom from stress. He was pleased that they accepted the prospect of tea with their grandmother with resignation if not with enthusiasm.

Tea passed without significant incident. In turn the children spoke of their schools and special interests, carefully edited to avoid irritating the old lady. The mill was not mentioned.

Dinner was much the same. Sparse, boring and over quickly.

Simon had already told his mother that they would be leaving next day. She had grumbled but could not refuse to let them go.

Simon went to her room next morning to say goodbye. Lady Ridgeworth was dressed for going out but did not offer to come down stairs to see them off. Her only comment was to say she would be writing to James.

Chapter 14

The party arrived back in Stroud in jubilant mood. The children dropped back into their usual routine as though the last two days had not happened. Maria did not ask if they had enjoyed themselves but she gave Simon a questioning look. He shook his head and mouthed, 'later.'

Later meant after the children had gone to bed. The three adults sat in the parlour and Simon told them about the Bath visit, leaving out some of the distressing details. Maria did not comment but James shook his head and said, 'She is a very unhappy lady.'

It was New Year's Eve and a small group of friends came to dinner and stayed until the clock struck twelve. None of the guests were used to late hours so they left as soon as the toasts had been drunk.

Simon enjoyed a further half hour with his brother and sister-in-law.

'Must you leave so soon?' James asked.

Simon nodded. He looked at his brother and said, quietly, 'I have some important matters to chase up. I have enjoyed being with you all and will try to see you again soon.'

Simon had decided to return to town by train. The weather sages predicted snow and he did not want to be stranded miles from anywhere. He trusted his coachman to find shelter if necessary and continue the journey when it was safe to do so. He was sorry to leave but had a strange, unidentified restlessness that made him eager to get back to normality.

Simon had said his private farewells but the whole family came out to wave him off. All three boys clamoured to accompany him to the station but James had solved the problem by ordering out the small trap he used for parish visits. 'There will not be room for of you. John will see your uncle on his way.'

Noakes had said his own goodbyes and waited until Simon and John were seated before he climbed up beside the driver.

As they waited on the platform, John said, 'I have thought about the talk we had. I talked to Grandpa and he said I would be a fool to miss the opportunity of going to university. He said the mill will still me mine one day. So, I will go when it is time. I just have to learn all I can about running the mill before I go. But please, if you can manage it, please try to have a son of your own.' Simon gave the boy a hug and said huskily, 'I am proud of you. I am sure you will manage any and all of the duties that fall to you. But I will bear your wishes in mind.' It was as far as he was prepared to go, even to please John.

As the train jerked into motion the first flakes of snow mingled with the smoke drifting past the windows. The semi-darkness seemed like a curtain being drawn between the past and the future. Simon sat back in his seat and smiled at his valet. 'I hear you have been adopted, *Uncle Noakes.*'

Noakes returned the smile. 'It is an honour. They are delightful children.' He sensed that his Lordship was in a confiding mood but was content to wait until he was asked a direct question. When it came, the question surprised Noakes out of his usual reticence.

'Do you ever miss not having had a family and children of your own?'

'Whatever for?!' Noakes exclaimed. In a more moderate tone he continued, 'I have no complaints, my Lord. I have been kept quite busy,' he finished with a chuckle.

'Point taken. I hope I have not been too much of a burden.' Noakes just shook his head and they lapsed into a comfortable silence.

Simon had a lot to think about. He had enjoyed a long talk with Mr Wallace and respected him for the way he had worked to create a thriving business from very humble beginnings. He wanted John to run it when he retired and had questioned Simon on what would be expected of the boy as a Viscount. It had been a very frank discussion. Wallace had listened and finally said, 'Sounds much like running the mill. Get competent staff and keep a check on them. There is no need to be there all the time.' He chuckled, 'Unless, like me you have nothing better to do.'

Simon was glad John had listened to his grandfather's advice and thankful that Wallace had given it. John had great responsibilities ahead of him and would need all the training he could get to carry both roles.

By the time they reached London everything was covered in a pristine white coat. Except the roads which had been turned into a muddy slush. Simon stepped gingerly down from the cab and hurried indoors. Immediately he was engulfed in the formality of life in a noble household. His outer clothes were taken away and refreshments served in his study.

His secretary had sorted his mail into separate piles and Simon dealt first with the more serious letters. Peters was very well organised and back correspondence was attached for reference. Simon only needed to made notes and allow his secretary to frame the replies. He authorised payment of the bills and dismissed his Peters with a few words of appreciation for work well done.

Simon next wrote personal letters to Truro and his family, thanking them for their hospitality and promising to visit again as soon as he could arrange it. The last few weeks had brought home to him how barren his life had become. He was always busy but he felt something was lacking. He was welcomed and respected wherever he went but there was nothing he really looked forward to with anticipation.

Reluctantly Simon opened the first of the invitations. Some he would have to accept but the thought gave him no pleasure. Most of his friends were still away from town but acquaintances, mostly female, were getting in ahead of the rush to secure his presence at up-coming events. It would be much worse when the Marriage Mart got into its stride. He was dreading the coming Season.

Simon was not vain but an unattached man of wealth and title was the main target for marriage minded ladies.

He was in a difficult position. His re-awakened libido was straining for release but, as yet, he had not met anyone he wanted to share it with. He was not looking for a wife and the thought of visiting a brothel filled him with revulsion. He needed a mistress, a discreet and accommodating woman who would accept that she was not to be included in his life any further than the necessary person services. The thought made Simon squirm. It diminished the woman as a person. He tried to reason that she would be under no obligation and his previous partners had appeared to enjoy their encounters.

Bea, who had been hovering at the back of his mind came into full focus. At least she had not invaded his dreams lately. Simon gave an irritable snort. Bea *was* a lady in all but name and therefore not a candidate for the post of mistress.

Why not? She is a widow in straightened circumstances and might be open to an offer.

His blood warmed at the prospect which was ridiculous. He did not know her beyond a couple of chance meetings. Bea, the child, had been intriguing, with a strong sense of right and wrong. He was sure she would roundly berate him if he suggested anything immoral. The Bea of his dreams had been alluring but he could not trust his memory of that one embrace to be anything more than wishful thinking. 'I have to find her first,' he answered the inner voice. It was too soon to expect to hear from Jones. He, or his son, had little to go on. Just a name and a vague destination. The seaside could be anywhere.

Simon thrust his wayward thoughts aside and went to change for dinner.

Over the next few weeks Simon immersed himself in meetings concerning the Reform Bill. He revised the speech he had drafted and practised it on Noakes. He did not expect or receive any comments but it helped to hear the words out loud. Any spare moments were filled with estate business, visits to his tailor, obligatory social occasions and anything else that should have kept his mind off Bea. She refused to budge, becoming clearer whenever he was in the company of other ladies.

It was well into March before Jones and Son were shown into his study. Simon ordered ale in preference to tea and told his butler he was not to be disturbed.

Jones junior handed over a bulky folder. 'It is all in their, My Lord but we thought you might have further instructions.'

Simon opened the folder. The papers were sorted into separate sections and it would take hours to digest it all. 'Have you found her?' he asked.

'Miss Hastings is living in a small village near Felixstowe.'

Simon did not register the name in his wonder at the destination. Felixstowe! He had been within a mile or two of her! Felixstowe was close to Alan's place near Ipswich.

Something in the older Jones voice alerted Simon that something was wrong. He asked for clarification.

By circuitous routes Jones junior had located people who knew Mrs Fleming in Cambridge. Most were in ignorance of her whereabouts but were eager to be helpful. The Hastings and Mr Fleming were respected locally although Mr Fleming did not spend much time in Cambridge. Jones had followed a lead to the registry office, found the address of Mr Fleming in Edinburgh and gone there.'

'What I found there was not good,' Jones said sadly. 'Fleming was already married at the time he went through a ceremony with Miss Hastings.'

Simon was stunned. A bigamous marriage was the last thing he could have expected.

'However,' Jones senior put in, 'our brief was to find Mrs Fleming.'

The younger Jones had retraced his steps to work on the less significant comments of his informants.

The owner of the company from which Mrs Fleming had hired a coach had a strange tale to tell. A young man had spoken to her immediately before she left and they had gone together to a nearby hotel for a short while. Then the driver had been told they were going to London. Half way there they stopped for the night and next morning the lady's luggage was transferred to the gentleman's coach and her driver dismissed. He had since left to take up other employment.

'The company's the owner could not remember the exact address as a small fire had destroyed some of his records. He suggested I find the firm that had taken her household possessions,' Jones concluded.

'That's it in a nutshell, my Lord,' the older Jones concluded. 'The lady is living under her maiden name and has a companion and a youth as general helper. She does not appear to be in need.'

Simon thanked them for a job well done and rang for them to be shown out. He was so shaken by the news he could not even get up from his chair.

He did not know how long he sat there before opening the file. The first paper only gave the address. Then came a whole ream of step-by-step actions with reference to statements in the third section. Last of all was Jones and Sons account. It was well within the amount Simon had paid them in advance. Simon closed the folder and placed it in his safe. He stared at the closed door, filled with profound disappointment.

That evening Simon only ate half of his dinner and retired to his library with a bottle of brandy.

Next morning Simon awoke with a headache, upset stomach and a bad temper.

He had dreamed about Bea again. It was not a sensual dream as she had just stood at a distance gazing at him sadly.

Blasted woman! Why wouldn't she leave him alone? He had done all he could. Whether from guilt or shame she had taken actions to conceal her destination so he could not even pay the intended compensation.

He got out of bed angrily. His movements were uncoordinated and he stubbed his toe on the bedframe. He swore when his fidgeting caused Noakes to nick his chin with the razor. He apologised immediately and grunted, 'A bad night,' by way of explanation.

There was no reasonable explanation for his erratic behaviour in the following days. He accepted invitations and flirted with willing women but although he was often tempted to take things further, he just could bring himself to follow it through.

The surge of physical desire took hold at inconvenient moments, usually after thinking about Bea. He could not get her out of his system. He felt betrayed and tried to tell himself all women were basically unfaithful. It was Monica all over again.

The absurdity finally brought him to his senses. How could she be unfaithful when they had never really met. Just a few minutes with a young girl and a chance collision in a crowded marketplace?

In desperation he locked himself in his study and read through the folder, word by word.

Two things stood out. Bea had married Fleming within days of her father's death. Had she married a much older man for security? It sounded reasonable.

Last year she had gone away with a young man. Again, when she was in need of help. Had she been having an affair while her husband was away for long periods? None of the statements mentioned visitors but it was not impossible. He did not know how long she had stayed with him before settling in Little Moorings. Had she been cast off when the younger man tired of her?

Either way she was not an innocent. He saw a way of getting her out of his system once and for all.

Noakes was getting worried. In his later years Lord Ridgeworth's father had lost his mind. Not violently, just a slow deterioration until he did not recognise his wife or son. Was his lordship going the same way? He was sure of it when his master rushed into the room and ordered, 'Pack a small bag. I am going to Felixstowe.' That gave Noakes a shock. Felixstowe was quite close to Ipswich. His lordship's confusion was worse than Noakes cared to believe. It was not his place to question his employer but was given no chance to probe as Ridgeworth left as swiftly as he had arrived muttering about train times.

Noakes automatically packed for himself as well on the assumption that he would be accompanying his employer. When they were ready to leave Simon saw Noakes handing his own bag to the cab driver.

Simon frowned. 'I did not ask you to company me.'

'But, my Lord, I always....'

Simon cut him short. 'I do not need a nursemaid. You are getting...' He could not finish the sentence. Noakes had served him faithfully all his adult life. At times they were almost friends but Noakes never took advantage. The man looked really upset at being left behind. 'Oh, get aboard or we will miss the train.

There was a press of people at the platform barrier. Lord Ridgeworth flashed the first-class ticket he had sent a footman to buy and strode forward. Hampered by the bags Noakes followed close behind with just a nod to the ticket inspector. He spent the entire journey worrying about what would happen at the other end when he was found to be travelling without a ticket. For the first time in his life he was breaking the law.

As expected, the Felixstowe inspector asked for Noakes' ticket. Lord Ridgeworth turned back, frowned and then laughed. He handed the inspector a coin and they were through.

'Sorry about that,' Ridgeworth said casually. 'I forgot.'

Yes, you did! Noakes thought. *'And what are you going to do when you realise we are at the wrong station?*

But it appeared Lord Ridgeworth really had meant to come to Felixstowe. Now Noakes was the one confused.

Ridgeworth ordered the cab driver to take them to a good hotel. He was shocked to be told there were no rooms available. He handed over his card and a shilling but the receptionist shook his head. 'I am sorry, Lord Ridgeworth, the Easter rush has started and we are fully booked.'

Simon stumbled to the door. He had never been turned away before. Even if a room had not been pre-booked his card and a tip always found that one was free.

Ridgeworth turned to his valet. 'Find somewhere else. I have a call to make.'

Another cab had just rolled up, its roof loaded with cases. A prosperous looking gentleman started to alight. Ridgeworth spoke a few words to him and marched away.

'How will he know where I am?' Noakes spoke aloud and received an odd look from two ladies just exiting the hotel.

Chapter 15

Bea had initially been disappointed to find that the rented cottage was not actually on the coast. She had been looking forward to seeing the sea.

The cottage was in fact a medium-sized house set in its own grounds. She had sent a letter to the letting agent to say she would be late arriving but had been unable to give an exact date. Bea collected the key from a neighbour as directed. It took a few minutes as the neighbour had much to say. 'I'm Mrs Potley, ma'am.' She told Bea she had lit the fires every other day to keep the house aired and did Miss Hasting want her to come in daily? Bea thanked her and said she would let her know later and went to inspect her new home.

The front door opened onto a square hall with doors on either side and a central staircase. Still wearing her hat and coat Bea looked into each room. They were a good size but too fussily furnished for her taste. The staircase was wide, stained on either side with a bare mid-section that suggested there used to be a carpet. With Dora following Bea climbed to the upper floor. Four doors here. Bea entered the one on the right. It overlooked the street and Bea was just in time to see Jane's carriage moving away. It seemed they would be staying here for at least one night. Bea had just decided it would do until she found something better when Dora called out, 'Come and look at this.'

Dora stood by the window in the rear bedroom. She had shed her cloak but still wore the satchel. Bea joined her and looked out. A river flowed just beyond the garden fence and she could see several small craft, both sail and oared, on the water. On the far side of the river was a wide towpath and beyond that a view of open fields. 'Just like Cambridge,' Dora sighed. 'Not that we had a garden or the river so close but you could see it every time we went to church or for a stroll.' Bea had not had much time for strolling and Dora could not see the point of walking just for the sake of it. But Bea understood what she meant.

She had missed the wide sky on her only walk in London. Even the park had a limited view. And Dora was right, it did have a comfortable feeling of home.

Freddie called up the stairs, 'Miss Bea, there's someone here to see you.'

Bea went down to meet an elderly lady carrying a large basket. She introduced herself as Mrs Cornish and said Mrs Potley had reported her arrival. 'I have come to welcome you and brought a few things to get you going.'

Bea recognised the name from the agent's letter. Mr Cornish owned much of the land including all the houses. Bea thanked the kind lady and Dora took the basket of groceries through to the kitchen. 'I won't keep you, my dear. We are just along the road. Please let us know if you need anything.' Bea thanked her and followed Dora into the kitchen.

Freddie had stacked their luggage in the hall and was in the kitchen inspecting the basket's contents. All the basics were there including a jug of milk. 'I found this on the table,' Dora said and handed Bea a neatly written list.

Welcome to Little Moorings, it began and was signed E.G. Cornish.

Mrs Potley is an honest and reliable cleaner. She also takes in laundry.

Milk, eggs and cheese were available at the farm, also poultry with advance notice.

The privy is emptied on Wednesday night.

An omnibus runs three times a week to Felixstowe and twice a week to Ipswich. Shops in both towns deliver.

Please ask me for any other information needed.

'How thoughtful,' Bea said with a slight lump in her throat. 'I wonder if the other neighbours are equally friendly.'

Dora frowned at Freddie. 'Just you remember what I said. No gossiping. We just came here after Mr Hastings died.'

Freddie shrugged, 'If you say so. I've had a look outside. Garden needs seeing too.'

Bea hid a smile. She had a feeling that they could settle here but she still did not want to reveal too much about her background.

Bea did buy the house. The tranquil setting was soothing after her weeks of worry. Dora and Freddie liked it too. The neighbours were friendly but not intrusive and it did not take long for them all to be absorbed into the small community. Apart from Mr and Mrs Cornish, the other inhabitants of the small hamlet were all manual workers. Bea was in a similar position to her status in Cambridge. She would have friendly neighbours but no real friends.

Out of politeness, Bea let it be let it be known that she had lost both parents in quick succession and needed a complete change of scene. It was true in a way and also gave a plausible reason for a lady of her age being unmarried. Bea did not like lying but a little evasion and suggestion quashed undue speculation.

The months passed. Bea had the house re-decorated and sent for her own furniture. She loved pottering in the garden with one of Mrs Potley's sons to do the heavy digging. Or sitting in the shade to watch the craft on the river. She particularly like watching the brightly painted barges and their patient horses as they carried goods between the coast and Ipswich. Dora found it easier to mix with the other women but her closest friend was the wife of Mr Cornish's farm manager who, like Bea and Dora, was in a mid-way class between the workers and the gentry. Freddie was friendly with everyone. He built a hen-run more for the fun of it than a need to economise and one of the other cottagers taught him to row a small dinghy and fish.

It was all very respectable and unthreatening. She tried not to think too much about the future. Bea had more time on her hands than ever before and bought a dog to accompany her on her solitary walks. 'We are all happy,' Bea told herself whenever her spirits sagged.

As summer faded into autumn Bea made an effort to explore further afield. With winter on the horizon she joined a lending library in Ipswich and stocked up on needles and wool and started on some tapestry cushions. And there was always her piano to play and evoke memories of happier days. The Cornish's took her to church each week and she was soon asked to play the piano when the regular pianist complained that it hurt his arthritic hands.

Bea was not unhappy but the prospect of drifting into a lonely old age was depressing.

One day in December, after a long spell of wet weather, Bea was walking around her bedraggled garden when she heard shouts and male laughter coming from the river. She moved to the bottom of the garden to see what was happening. A little down river a good-looking man in a rowing boat had become entangled in a fishing net thrown over the back of a barge. There was another rowing boat but the man was bent double laughing so she only saw a flash of fair hair.

Her heart beat faster as she thought of Simon Armitage. Turning away quickly she berated herself for still thinking about him and went indoors.

One day, just before Easter, Bea was in her garden. Everything was sprouting as the days lengthened and would soon gladden her heart with colour.

She had been here for nearly a year. It had not been boring exactly but nothing of note had happened. 'You should be thankful for that,' she told herself sternly. Jane wrote to her frequently but it was like reading a book about a different universe.

Freddie, who had been cleaning the front windows, came around the side of the house and handed Bea a small card. Before she had a chance to read it Freddie said, 'There's a swell gent at the front who says he's Viscount Ridgeworth.'

'What is he doing here?'

'Don't know. He just asked if you were in and could he speak to you.'

Bea glanced down at the mud on her dress and the boots she wore in the garden. 'Show him into the parlour and close the door. I need to get upstairs to make myself presentable.'

Bea kicked off her boots on the back step and waited just inside the kitchen until she heard the parlour door close. Freddie grinned at her as she scooted up the stairs.

A little later Bea hesitated outside the parlour door. While she changed into a modest but pretty gown of fine wool her mind had been racing. Why was Lord Ridgeworth here? How had he found her? Why had he come in person?

Bea took a deep breath and opened the door and froze. Simon! She recognised him instantly. 'Simon,' she whispered in a mixture of delight, shock and confusion. She had not looked at the card after Freddie told her the caller's name. It was in the pocket of the apron she had torn off as she ran up the stairs.

He stood up from petting her dog and took a step towards her.

'Bea,' he said softly, taking another step towards her. 'You recognise me?' The woman of his dreams was even lovelier in the flesh. Her simple gown revealed soft, feminine curves that set his pulse racing.

Simon's smile turned Bea's bones to jelly. 'Please sit down,' she said more for her own benefit than politeness. She did not want to fall at his feet. Bea flopped inelegantly onto the sofa and Simon sat opposite. They gazed at each other until Bea managed to gather enough wits to offer him refreshment.

'Not just now but I have a cab waiting. Perhaps your man can see to the driver. You will return to talk to me?' he added anxiously as Bea got to her feet. She nodded and raced from the room before he could see her blush.

Freddie was waiting in the hall, agog with curiosity. She gave brief instructions before he could ask questions and turned back to the parlour. Her head told her not to go back inside. Her heart took charge of her feet.

Simon was still petting the dog. 'You will be covered in hairs,' she said inanely. She could feel the heat rising in her cheeks again so she grabbed Scamps' collar and thrust him into the hall. In that few seconds Simon had stood up. Light from the window turned his hair into a shining halo but put his face in the shade.

'Why are you here?' Bea asked.

Simon shook his head. 'I don't really know. I have been so worried about you. I had to make sure you were safe after you were thrown out of your home.'

Bea covered her mouth with her hands and stared at him in horror. Dear God, he had been to Cambridge. What did he know?

Simon moved to crouch down in front of her and took hold of her hands. It was an intimate gesture but it felt so natural.

Bea felt faint, unsure if it was from shock or the feel of his hands gently holding hers. She was slowly swaying towards him before she came to her senses. 'How did you find me?'

He saw her fear. 'Don't worry. Your secret is safe with me.'

Bea tugged her hands free. 'But how did you find me?!' Her voice had risen and Scamp barked and scratched at the door. Scamp's continual barking made her pull away. She could not look at him. What would he think of her?

Bea jerked upright and onto her feet almost knocking him off balance. From a safe distance she asked again, 'Why are you here?'

Simon stood but did not come any closer. 'Please sit down and listen to me.'

Against her better judgement Bea did as he asked and listened while he told her how she had been found. 'They are honest men and will not tell a soul.'

'How much do you know?'

'Probably most of it. I sent them to find one of my abused tenants. I was shocked when I heard you are not really Mrs Fleming.'

'Don't call me that. I have left that person behind. I just want to stay here safe and quiet.' She was unaware that the tears were streaming down her face.

It was too much for Simon to bear. He shifted until he was perched on the edge of the sofa and gathered her into his arms and, Glory Be! she did not resist. It felt so right. It was not lust. It was not even desire. It was a need. A need to hold and cherish. 'I will always take care of you,' he whispered as his hand slid up to touch the bare skin of her neck.

Bea wanted to stay like this forever. She could feel his heart beating and smell cologne and something else, something that made her head swim. The warmth of his hand on her neck coincided with Dora's angry voice and Simon's last words penetrated.

Bea jerked herself free so suddenly she stumbled and Simon made a grab for her arm but she tugged it free and moved to stand with her back to the empty fireplace. She drew on every shred of pride and said coldly, 'Whatever you have been told I am not a loose woman.'

It was so close to his reason for coming that Simon was filled with shame and he flushed violently.

Dora burst into the room, took in Bea's defensive stance and the man's red face and rushed to stand between them. 'I don't know why you are here but if you don't want to walk back to wherever you have come from you had better leave now!'

The dog was tugging at his trouser leg, the breathless virago's stare should have drawn blood and the young man in the doorway had his fists raised. 'I can explain' Simon started to say but was cut short.

'You can explain to the cabbie why you are keeping him from his dinner!'

Simon looked at Bea and his heart cracked. Although she was still standing, she looked broken, almost lifeless. He could not bear it and took a step forward. The angry woman's hands landed on his chest and the man grabbed his arm. The dog got under his feet and they were all in danger of falling to the floor.

'Bea!' he cried, as he was hustled from the room.

He could have resisted but fighting with her servants would not make Bea listen. Chastened, embarrassed and confused he allowed the young man to shove him into the cab and the door slammed before he was settled on the seat. Through the hatch in the roof the cabbie was saying something about his dinner being ruined and it was going to cost him.

Simon did not care. He did not care that he had been man-handled by servants. He did not care that a dog had torn his trousers. He did not care that he was crying.

The short ride was hardly long enough for Simon to pull himself together. He had never felt so wretched or ashamed. 'Where to?' demanded the voice above his head.

Where to? It dawned on Simon that he had no idea where to find Noakes. He did not even remember the name of the hotel that had turned him away. With an effort he said, 'The best hotel.'

The hotel considered the best by the cabbie was not the one where he had last seen Noakes. Simon told the cabbie to wait and went inside and spoke to the receptionist. Noakes had not registered here. He went back to the cab. 'The next best. This one is full.' Growling and muttering the driver moved further down the street.

'Right one or not, you can get out here. I want my dinner and I don't want a crazy passenger!'

Simon tried to gather his dignity and got down from the cab. He handed the cabbie a handful of coins and said, 'I am sorry I kept you so long.'

'Crazy. Crazy and too rich to care where he throws his money,' the cabbie gloated as he examined the coins. 'Gee up laddie, we'll eat well tonight!' The words faded into the distance and Simon stood in the middle of the pavement not knowing what to do next.

People passed him on either side, giving him censorious looks and a wide berth. He looked up and down the street in the vain hope that Noakes would suddenly appear.

Before he could decide which way to go, a grubby urchin rushed up. 'Are you Lord Riddwigs?' The boy was still trying to get his tongue around Ridgeworth when he was pushed aside by an older, better dressed youth who bowed and said, 'Lord Ridgeworth, I presume.'

The first boy protested, 'I saw him first!' 'The larger boy's arrogant 'So?'' made him step back snivelling something about fairness.

Simon was too relieved to care. Here was someone who knew him. He nodded to the winner but was given no time to ask questions.

'Please follow me, my Lord. Your man is just over there.' With a wave of his hand, the boy indicated across the street to where Noakes was pacing outside a hotel door. By virtue of size and arrogant manner his saviour stopped the traffic and led Simon across the road, trailed by the whining urchin. Noakes rushed to meet him midway much to the annoyance of drivers.

'My Lord!' Noakes gasped, 'You are safe!' He started to say he had engaged rooms but was interrupted by the angry demand, 'What about our money?!'

Simon reached into his pocket for the small change he carried for tips. It was sadly depleted since he had paid the cabbie but he tipped the remaining coins into the boy's outstretched hand.

The boys looked at it in contempt. 'He promised us more us more than that!'

Angry shouts alerted Noakes to the fact that they were still standing in the middle of the road. He hurried them on to the pavement saying, 'You will all be paid. Wait here.'

As Noakes shepherded him across the lobby, Simon roused himself enough to think 'all' was a rather exaggerated description. His senses had almost recovered by the time they reached a privacy of a bedroom. 'I was so worried.' Noakes was babbling about sending boys to watch every hotel in Felixstowe. He looked more dishevelled than Simon had ever seen him and kept patting his master on his shoulders and arms.

Simon shrugged him off and frowned. 'You have been behaving very oddly of late, Noakes.'

'I could say the same of you! You have not been yourself for some time and I...' Noakes stopped abruptly. He had just reprimanded his employer and almost accused him of losing his mind. 'Beg pardon, my Lord, I...

This time he was cut short by an urgent knocking on the door. It opened to reveal and agitated porter. 'There's a mob of boys causing a disturbance downstairs,' he said to Noakes. 'You had better come and sort it out before we call a constable.' Noakes begged Simon's pardon again and fetched a purse from his own bag that stood by the door. He followed the porter out and Simon sat down on the side of the bed.

He was still there when Noakes returned.

It took time and some very candid exchanges to sort things out. Noakes had never taken advantage of Simon's trust before and it shook them both. Simon took an honest look at his recent behaviour and decided Noakes was justified in talking to him like a worried parent. It was his turn to apologise.

The only thing Simon did not mention was Bea's bigamous marriage. 'I have to see her again. To explain how I feel.' Noakes raised an eyebrow and Simon huffed. 'You are right. I don't know how I feel. It is like nothing I have ever felt before.'

He is in love, Noakes thought sadly. He had observed the condition in other men and was grateful he had never been infected. He reassured himself that it seldom lasted and he had never known it to be fatal. But he had already overstepped and suggested a hot bath and a meal might make his lordship feel better.

It did to some extent. At least it gave Simon time to marshal his thoughts.

He sent Noakes away and lay on the bed, staring at the ceiling. What he felt for Bea confused him. He wanted her physically but it was more than that. He had wanted Monica. She had teased him into a state of painful arousal and he had strutted like a peacock when she agreed to marry him. He had captured the prize of the season. *And what did you really get?* His inner voice taunted. *It was not a broken heart.* 'I never loved her,' he said aloud, amazed that he had never realised it before. He also realised that he had never actually proposed. Monica had said he could not have her until they were married. Then her mother had rushed into the room, accusing him of seducing her daughter. What a fool he had been. He had been blinded by an accomplished flirt and made to pay the price.

That was not how he felt about Bea.

Simon sat up so abruptly his head swam. Good God! He loved Bea! He needed her like a drowning man needs air to survive! But that still did not define his feelings. He also needed to make her happy to make her feel safe and cherished. He wanted her to love him.

He went to the table and reached for paper and a pen. The letter took him far into the night as he explained all he had done to find her. He had not been searching for Mrs Fleming or even Miss Hastings. He had been frantic to find Bea, the girl who had talked to him about the unfairness of people being condemned without a fair trial. It had amused him at the time but her sincerity had taken root in his heart. Why had he never realised she was the catalyst that changed him from a hedonistic youth into a responsible and caring man? She was the reason why he now fought for the rights of the under-dog.

She had made him the man he was!

I love her, he murmured as he finally fell into an exhausted sleep.

Chapter 16

Bea couldn't sleep. The events of the afternoon kept replaying in her mind like actors on a stage.

She had been shocked and then delighted when she discovered that Lord Ridgeworth and Simon Armitage were the same person. He remembered her and had tried to find her. She was worried about that. More and more people knew of her whereabouts. The chance of someone making the connection to her scandalous marriage was a constant dread.

He had held her in his arms and she had soared to Heaven only to be thrust out when she understood he was making her an improper proposal. She did not know what she would have done if Dora and Freddie had not thrown him out. As much as she loved him, she could not betray her own honour by becoming his mistress.

Oh, why did he have to come when she had found some peace?

His hat and gloves were still on the hall table. At times she wanted to stamp them into the ground. At others she wanted to hold them to her breast and pretend he was coming back to …. Make his offer clear? Michael had said Lord Ridgeworth was married. She was not going down that route again no matter how much it would hurt to send him away.

Dora had not known who he was when she ordered Lord Ridgeworth from the house and unrepentant when she found out. Bea knew she ought to be grateful for such staunch support. Freddie had wanted to go after Lord Ridgeworth and give him what for! Even Scamp had tried to defend her.

Bea was too miserable to cry. But she hurt. Deep inside where she kept her love for Simon.

It had taken a long time to calm Dora down. She had berated all men and Lord Ridgeworth in particular. They were all selfish, immoral and guilty of any other crime Dora could think of. 'If he hadn't sold the shops and had renewed the leases we could have stayed where we were and you would not be wasting your youth in this backwater.'

'Dora, that is another matter entirely. You know we could not have stayed in Cambridge,' Bea said reasonably. 'He came to make sure I was safe.'

'I don't know how you can defend him. A married man making improper advances.'

Bea could because she loved him. She would always love him even if she never saw him again. And she was too tired to argue. Her only escape was to say she had a headache and retire to her room without any dinner.

By the next morning Bea's headache was real. Dark circles under her eyes and a pale face had Dora fussing over her until she wanted to scream. They usually went into Felixstowe on a Saturday to shop for the weekend but Bea did not know where Simon was staying. She could not cope with seeing him again so soon. Dora refused to go in case Ridgeworth returned so Freddie was sent off with a list.

Bea drifted around the house and garden, starting a job and abandoning it a few moments later. It was a long day.

When Freddie returned, he handed Bea a letter he had taken from the postman at the bus stop to save the man trudging to Bea's end of the village. 'It's from that lord,' Freddie growled. 'I wanted to throw it in the privy.'

Bea took it out to her favourite seat in the garden and just held it in her lap, staring at the bold, black writing. Part of her wanted to rip open the envelope to see what he had to say and part was scared that it would weaken her resolve to put him out of her mind. With a sigh she acknowledged the latter was impossible and broke the seal.

The letter was several pages long and began with the simple salutation 'Bea'. He apologised for his behaviour yesterday. Then there was a long explanation of why he had been desperate to see her. It was a bit garbled, jumping from his visit to Cambridge to the investigators report, a reference to her sense of justice and back to statements from her neighbours. 'When I saw you today and knew none of those reasons were true. I have never forgotten you although I was not aware of it. How else could my dreams a have been so vivid?' Bea frowned. What dreams? And, how vivid? 'I have been in limbo for so many years. Seeing you has brought me back to life.'

The letter ended with a plea for another meeting, which sounded humble, and a statement not to deny him or he might come uninvited.

It was signed, 'Your obedient servant forever, Simon Armitage.'

Bea did not know what to think. Obedient servant did not sound like someone who threatened to ignore her wishes. At that moment she wished her Papa was alive. His advice had always been sound even if it was not what she wanted to hear. Bea shook her head at her own silliness. If Papa was still alive the last four years would have been entirely different.

Even so, she closed her eyes and whispered, 'Papa what should I do?' Like many such questions the answer came from her own nature. The lesser risk was to meet him somewhere public where they would both have to act with decorum. If he came back to the house uninvited, she could not vouch for his safety.

Bea looked up and was irritated to see Dora watching from the kitchen window and Freddie pretending to tidy the wood pile. She had never needed to remind them that they were servants. Indeed, she did not think of them as such. She knew they loved her and she loved them as family but in this she would do what she thought was right.

Bea got up and beckoned Freddie to follow her into the kitchen. 'Lord Ridgeworth has requested another meeting.' Bea raised her hand to stop any protests. 'I will see him in a public place and hear what he has to say. We will not discuss this again.'

She felt mean speaking to them in such a way but it had to be done.

Bea wrote to Simon at the address on the hotel notepaper saying she would meet him on Tuesday morning at 11.am on the footpath behind her house. The local postal service was very prompt, if it was collected early on Monday morning, there was not collection on Sundays, he should get it first thing on Tuesday morning. She dared not suggest later in the week because he might arrive unexpectedly. The two days between would give her time to calm down and bolster her resolve.

The rest of the day was strained but Bea could not suppress the little spark of joy that she would see Simon again soon.

On Sunday morning Bea sent Freddie with a note to Mr and Mrs Cornish that she was feeling a little unwell and would not be going to church. She asked them to give her apologies to the vicar for not being available to play the piano.

The rest of the day and the one following passed on leaden feet.

Simon woke late on Saturday but was in no hurry to get out of bed. He could not expect a reply from Bea until Monday at the earliest. Noakes brought his breakfast and they went through the usual routine of washing, shaving and dressing. He alarmed Noakes by saying he was going to ride over to see Truro. 'I will stay the night and maybe Sunday, too.' The horror on his valet's face made him laugh. 'No, you do not need to come with me. I am old enough, and sane enough,' he stressed, 'to be let out alone. You can take this letter and have it sent by special delivery.'

Simon hired a horse from a local stable and asked directions to Ipswich, avoiding the main road. They were easy to follow and took him along the tow-path beside the river. He slowed as he came abreast of Bea's house but he could not see any movement at the windows or in the neatly kept garden. It was fortunate that the river was too wide to jump or he might have given in to the urge to see Bea again. Or perhaps not. He had to give her a chance to refuse. He rode on hoping a few his days with Alan and the children would keep him from going mad with frustration.

He did not need to give Alan a specific reason for his impromptu visit. A vague suggestion of business in the area was accepted without comment. The children were pleased to see him and, as it was a fine day, soon had him out in the garden for a game they called cricket. It was more like a three-person game of bat and ball as he was to be Sarah's helper. He bent over the little girl and took the weight of the bat as Alan and Lionel threw gentle balls towards her. Then they missed the clumsy returns so Simon could pick her up and run to the other end of the short pitch. When it was his turn Lionel played to win, hitting the ball accurately and sending the two adults to all corners of the garden. It was more fun than Simon had ever imagined.

He did not think of Bea for several hours.

In the comfortable privacy of Alan's library after dinner, his friend asked, 'Something bothering you, old chap?'

Simon said, 'I am in love,' before he could think the better of it. He then had to field Alan's questions, promising his friend would be the first to know if the lady accepted him. 'I hope the lady will be the first,' Alan chortled and changed the subject.

Sunday was taken up by a long ride in the morning, playing with the children in the afternoon and a cheerful dinner with some old friends Alan had already invited. Bea was never far from his thoughts and her presence in his dreams was nebulous, more a sense than actual happenings.

On Monday morning Alan slapped Simon on the back and said best of luck before he rode back to Felixstowe along the main road.

One more day, Simon told himself. Surely Bea would not keep him waiting for a reply. He was delighted to find Bea's reply was already waiting for him at the hotel. Simon tore open the envelope half dreading her refusal to see him. 'Tomorrow,' he sighed with relief. Bea would see him tomorrow. He checked his watch. Just twenty hours until he saw her again. He was too impatient to sit still so he went off to explore the town and the busy docks.

Simon dreamed of Bea again that night. Not an erotic dream but she came willingly into his arms and he was filled with contentment.

Next morning, he walked to Bea's hamlet. He did not want to cause talk by having a cab standing outside her house. And taking a horse posed the problem of where to leave it. He arrived at the meeting place much too early and he had checked his watch three times before he saw her walking towards him. He went to meet her with his hands outstretched, trying not to break into a run.

Chapter 17

Bea set out to meet Simon with a firm resolve to hear what he had to say and then send hm away. It would be hard but they could not have a respectable relationship and she could not be his mistress.

As Simon came forward to meet her with outstretched hands, she could not resist him. Her hands came up to meet his and he held them against his chest. She felt the warmth of his hands through her cotton gloves and saw the longing in his eyes. 'Bea,' he whispered as he lowered his head and his lips met hers.

It was a gentle kiss, almost reverent but it was her first real kiss and she returned it with an ardour she had not known she possessed. He drew back and looked into her eyes which were wide with wonder and her lips parted on a soft, 'Oh.' Simon had to restrain the urge to crush her in his arms and kiss her senseless.

The path was too narrow for them to walk abreast but he kept hold of her hand and led her back to a stile partially hidden behind some bushes. They sat down and he spoke the words in his heart. 'Bea, I love you. Please say you will marry me!'

He sounded so sincere that Bea felt her eyes fill with tears. She tried to pull her hands free and stand but he did not let her go.

'Please.'

The one word was enough to make Bea forget most of her sensible resolve but enough remained for her to move as far away from him as the wooden step allowed. She could not look at him as she said, sadly, 'I cannot. You know I cannot. You are already married.'

Simon frowned. Oh, lord! He ought to have told her about Monica before he proposed.

'I'm not! Not now.' Bit by bit he told her all the sordid details of his marriage. It did not show him in a very good light. He had married on a wave of lust. Was Bea thinking him too easily led by his urges? To mitigate his past behaviour he added, 'My parents were in favour of the match. I was the heir and they had been urging me to marry for some time. In their defence I have to say they did not know about the child.'

'Tell me about her. What is she like?'

Simon wished she had not asked. Since being with his family he had felt guilty for not taking interest in the child. He kept putting off a visit on the grounds of more pressing matters. 'She lives with her maternal grandmother,' he said cautiously.

'And?' Bea prompted. Simon could feel himself sinking further in Bea's regard but knew she was not going to be put off. He had to admit he did not see her. 'I sent Christmas gifts.' It sounded lame even to his own ears and Bea's disapproval was justified.

'None of it was the child's fault. She will grow up thinking she is unloved.'

In a desperate attempt to change the subject, Simon asked, 'Is that how you felt when that bounder Fleming deceived you?'

Bea actually smiled. 'Rob was not all bad. He did love me in a way, just as I loved him. He was like an uncle, a friend I had known all my life. He married me when I had just lost my father. Your agent, Tanner, was threatening to throw me out and I did not know what to do. I was confused and desperate. Rob rescued me!'

That did not make sense. She had married Fleming more the three years ago. 'Why didn't you appeal directly to me?'

Bea stamped her foot. 'I did not know you were Lord Ridgeworth!'

'Is that why you went off to London with that young man? Because you were desperate? Did he make you promises he did not keep?'

Bea stared at him in outraged shock. 'Certainly not! He is my cousin. He took me to stay with his mother!'

Simon apologised, filled with shame. Her going away with an unknown man had been the spur that had sent him rushing to Felixstowe to see if she might be open to a discreet liaison. He could not tell her that and went back to his original declaration. 'I love you, Bea. I did not realise why I was so desperate to find you. You have always been at the back of my mind.'

Bea argued that she had only been a child when he came to her father's shop. 'The only other time we met you did not even recognise me.'

Simon risked putting an arm around her shoulders and smiled. 'Perhaps not immediately. We did not have time to speak, but you were not a child in my dreams. Bea, I love you and want to marry you. To be with you forever.'

They argued. Bea cited the fear of her secret being discovered. Simon said that was unlikely.

'If you could find me so too can other people. I will not involve you in my scandal.'

'My past is not free of scandal but I survived. You were the innocent party and, whatever happens, we will deal with it together.'

'Yes, but if I am not a widow I will be judged on my morals. No-one will believe Rob and I were never intimate. He stayed in my house. We were seen out together.'

Simon did not hear her last words. He heart had soared at the knowledge that the marriage had never been consummated. He hated the thought of another man touching her but could have accepted it as she had believed herself married. He wanted her in all ways and not just for an affair. He loved her, had carried her in his heart for so many years without knowing why no other woman would do.

She wanted him too. He had seen the love in her eyes and he would be honoured to call her his wife.

A dog, not her own, ran up to Bea with lolling tongue and wagging tail. He was closely followed by a working man with a lumpy sack thrown over his shoulder. 'Afternoon, Miss Hastings.' He gave Simon a sideways glance.'

Bea eased herself away from Simon's embrace and bent to pet the dog. The man grinned. 'Sorry to disturb you but I have come to cut back these bushes.'

'Then we will get out of your way.' Bea rose and stepped forward with the dog frisking around her. She was very close to the water's edge and Simon went quickly to her side. She started to walk away and the man turned his interested gaze on Simon. 'Nice afternoon for a walk, sir.' The accompanying wink suggested other pleasures to be had in a concealed nook. Simon gave him a curt nod and followed Bea.

'That will be all around the village by nightfall,' Bea hissed over her shoulder when they were out of earshot.' Your cab at my door has already been mentioned.'

'Tell them we are about to be married. They will love it.'

Bea turned angrily. 'I fell into one disastrous marriage without proper thought. I will not make the same mistake twice!'

'But you love me.'

Bea could not deny it. She had already allowed him liberties and kisses. Either she loved him or she was a shameless hussy. 'Yes,' she whispered. 'Once and for always.'

Simon closed the gap between them and took her into his arms. The kiss swept them both away. Bea's hands came up to cradle his face and he lowered one hand to her bottom and pulled her closer to his arching groin.

A long, two-note whistle jerked Bea back to reality and she hid her face against Simon's chest. He gave the bargee on the other side of the river a casual wave of acknowledgement. When the barge was safely past, Simon tilted Bea's chin until she could not avoid his eyes. 'You will have to marry me now, Miss Hastings.'

Bea returned his smile and against all reason said, 'Yes.' They kissed again with less fervour but more ...., something. A promise? A commitment? Trust? Whatever it was it felt right.

Bea finally sighed. 'But we can't stand here in full view for all to see.' Unable to break away completely, Bea took his hand and, on the way to her back gate, they decided how to break the news. He learned that Dora and Freddie were almost family and knew all about her past. 'They have stood by me and I will not let them be pushed aside.'

Chapter 18

Bea and Simon entered the house through the kitchen door. Dora looked up from taking a pie from the oven. One glance at their linked hands and Bea's glowing smile told her more than she wanted to know. With a sigh she placed the hot dish on one side.

Freddie was less perceptive. He charged around the table and glared at Simon. 'Stay right there! I'll fetch your hat.' Bea grabbed his sleeve but was looking at Dora as she announced, 'We are going to be married.'

Simon ought to have been annoyed by the lad's, 'What him!' and the maid's sullen shake of her head but they had already demonstrated their affection and loyalty so he let the impertinence pass. Indeed, at that moment he felt more like a schoolboy called up before the headmaster for some misdemeanour. The maid muttered something that sounded like, 'We have heard that before,' had Bea rushing to his defence.

'It is not like that. Come into the parlour. We have a lot to tell you.' Simon wanted to protest but he had no authority in this house and did not want to sound domineering.

Bea led the way to the front room. She drew Simon to sit beside her on the sofa while the maid perched on the edge of the chair opposite. The lad stood at her shoulder with arms folded.

'I will take care of Bea,' Simon began trying to ignore their sceptical glances.

Bea patted his hand and said, 'Simon is not married.' Simon hardly said a word as Bea told of their meetings long ago and feelings they had been obliged to suppress. It was not the whole truth but near enough not to be a lie. Bea concluded her account by saying, 'Please be happy for me.'

'There will be a lot to arrange,' Simon told them. He cleared his throat and turned to Bea. 'Will your cousin allow you to be married from his house?'

Bea looked surprised. 'I thought we could be quietly married here.'

'No,' Simon replied with gentle firmness. 'We will be married with as much fanfare as we can manage. We have nothing to be ashamed of.'

'I have,' Bea insisted. 'What about the gossip?'

'The best way to avoid speculation is to give the gossips something else to talk about.'

'He's right, love,' Dora agreed. 'People mostly see what is thrust under their noses.' She frowned at Simon, 'How will you explain the sudden wedding?'

'As Bea just said, we have known and loved each other for years.' He smiled at Bea and squeezed her hand. 'Previous marriage vows have kept us apart for too long. Now we are both free, we want to be together as soon as possible.' It was near enough to his previous excuses to sound true.

'It could work,' Bea said. 'Jane and her family know we were both married but only Jane knows mine was not real.' She bit her lip and looked at Simon. 'My cousin Violet is not going to be pleased. She wanted you for herself.'

Simon frowned. 'I can't remember that I ever met her.'

Bea reminded him of their brief encounter.

'I don't remember it.'

'She is very beautiful,' Bea prompted.

Simon shrugged. 'I must have met scores of beautiful women but none as lovely as you.' Bea knew it could not be true but she was glad Simon thought so.

Dora stood up. This was getting too personal. 'I'll go and check on supper.' She signalled Freddie to join her and stopped at the door when Bea asked Simon to stay for the meal. At his assent Dora had a naughty hope that he would find it a disappointment. 'Freddie can clear the dining room while I find some serving dishes.'

Bea was not having that. They always ate in the kitchen. It was more convenient and she had never dined alone. What could Simon say but 'Yes,' when asked if he would mind.

It was a novel experience to be served rabbit pie and plain, boiled vegetables straight from the saucepan. It was almost like being back in Stroud although James' servants were not so assertive. Freddie asked how Simon had got there and laughed when he said he had walked. 'Well, mind you don't fall in the river on the way back.'

Simon glanced at the window. The sun was low in the sky, leaving a pearly twilight. He had not realised how long they had been talking.

He left, reluctantly, as soon as the meal was finished. He thanked Dora and said he had enjoyed the meal, surprised to find that it was true and not just politeness.

Bea accompanied him to the garden gate. His farewell was more than words and Bea was flushed and slightly rumpled when she finally watched him walk away.

Dora had more to say when they were alone. 'Bea, do you really think you are doing the right thing? You hardly know him.'

'I know him in here,' Bea touched her breast. 'Simon has never been far from my thoughts. I really do love him, Dora. And Simon has always loved me, but, like most men I have heard of, took a long time to realise it.'

It was quite dark when Simon, rather footsore, reached his hotel. His shoes were not designed for long distance walks. He had hardly noticed the pain until he stopped walking as his head was too full of wonderment at knowing Bea loved him.

Noakes greeted him with relief and said he was glad his lordship had retrieved his hat. The relief vanished when his master flopped back on the bed with a silly grin on his face. 'You may congratulate me, Noakes. I am going to marry Miss Hastings.' Noakes was shocked out of his usual reticent and exclaimed, 'My lord, you hardly know the woman!'

Ridgeworth sat bolt upright and glared. 'Lady, Noakes! Miss Hastings is a lady.'

'I beg pardon my lord but isn't this rather sudden?'

Ridgeworth relaxed. 'I think I have known her all my life, even before we met.' Simon looked at his loyal servant. 'You know me better than anyone. Did you never wonder why I did not take up the lures thrown at me? I have been searching for Bea. No-one else has every touched my heart. Monica addled my senses for a while but I never loved her.'

Noakes nodded silently. He had been the recipient of his lordship's confidences so often. The euphoria of his brief engagement. The crushing disillusion of his marriage, quickly followed by the death of his beloved father. He had never met Miss Hastings and what he had heard of her did not sound promising. He prayed she was not another scorpion disguised as a butterfly.

Simon visited Bea again next day. They walked the river path but could not find another secluded spot so they went back to the cottage and shut themselves in the parlour – to discuss things. Only the thought of Dora rushing in with a rolling pin kept Simon from making love to Bea on the carpet. Even so he managed to give her a foretaste of the delights of a true marriage.

He had come on horseback this time and his mount was helping himself to Bea's flowers in the rear garden while Simon shared another simple meal around the kitchen table. This one was more relaxed but Bea's servants were still suspicious.

Simon was not sure he wanted to live under Dora Cotton's critical gaze. He accepted that she loved Bea like a mother loves a daughter but she would have to learn to treat him with more respect. Her last words to him the previous evening had been a command to never let Bea down. Her straight look had implied he would have her to deal with if he ever hurt her beloved mistress.

'You will always be welcome in my house, Mrs Cotton,' he had replied formally and then grinned. 'As my almost mother-in-law, perhaps I may be allowed to call you Dora.'

Dora had swatted him on the arms and said, 'Get away with you,'

Restrained by the thought of interruption, the lovers spent their time catching up on the events of the missing years. Simon cringed every time Bea mentioned Rob. Reason told him Fleming was a part of her life as much as Monica was part of his.

They came close to quarrelling when Bea asked if his daughter would live with them after their marriage.

'She is not my daughter!'

'She is an innocent child!' Bea watched his face although his head was bent and she could not see his eyes. His body spoke his thoughts. Disgust had held him rigid. Her censure had slumped his shoulders. Bea could not bear to see him shamed and placed a hand on his arm. 'I am sorry I have offended you but the case still stands. I think I have a right to know what part the….. you never did tell me her name…. the child will have in my life.'

Simon wanted to say she need never see Monica's daughter. But society knew of the child's existence. Sending her to live with her grandmother had been seen as logical at the time. Girls in general were not highly regarded until they were of marriageable age but most widowers remarried to provide a mother for their children. He did not care what people thought of him but Bea was vulnerable. He did not want her to be seen as a cruel, uncaring step-mother.

'Must we discuss it now? I will take you to meet her before we decide.'

'Her name?' Bea prompted, determined to make Simon see the little girl as a person and not just a reminder of her mother.

'It's Cynthia. I am not proud of the fact that I insisted on the name. I meant the sound of it to remind Monica of her perfidy. She just laughed and called me a fool.'

'Oh, Simon,' Bea rested her head against his shoulder. 'We all do things on the spur of the moment that we regret later.' She gave a bitter laugh. 'Look where it got me.'

It was Simon's turn to comfort. 'Eventually, it got you here, where you belong.' He suited words to actions and took her into his arms. They did not kiss. This was a moment of connection, a silent commitment that could not be put into words or blurred by passion. With his cheek resting on her hair, Simon accepted Bea's love as a wonderous gift. She could see his faults, would try to help him overcome them and love him even if he failed.

Once and for always, Bea had told him. She had meant 'forever' but she also loved him 'in all ways.' He would strive to his last breath to deserve her.

The intense moment passed and he kissed her.

That, too, passed far too quickly. He had things to do. Commitments he had forgotten in his haste to see her. And he had a marriage to arrange.

Bea gave him the letter she had written to Jane. It was long and disjointed but she knew Jane would understand. 'I will take this to Mrs Hastings myself,' Simon told her when it was time for him to leave. He smiled ruefully. 'I hope she receives the news better than Dora and Freddie.'

Jane responded to Bea's letter by coming to Little Moorings in person. She had been impressed by Lord Ridgeworth's manner when he delivered the letter but was worried by the speed of their decision to wed. Bea had said she had never met Ridgeworth and there had certainly been no mention at all of a Simon and a long acquaintance.

Bea greeted her friend warmly and the ladies retired to the parlour.

'Bea, don't you think you are being a little rash? What do you really know about Lord Ridgeworth?

'I love him and I know he loves me,' Bea replied with a dreamy smile. 'I probably did not explain it very well in my letter.

A detailed explanation carried them through the afternoon. Finally, Jane was reassured and really, she had no right to try to influence Bea one way or the other. She took a copy of that morning's Times from her bag and opened it at the announcements page. 'Lord Ridgeworth did not waste any time in announcing your betrothal.'

Simon had been very careful of the wording of the notice. There was no mention of Bea's marital status, just her name and 'daughter of John Hastings Esq. (dec'd).

'Ridgeworth made a formal call on Michael before he gave me your letter. It was a thoughtful gesture and did more for Michael's esteem than all the Trustees' lectures put together.'

'I agree,' Bea replied. 'It was not really necessary as I am of age but Michael is my closest male relative. I would like him to stand in my father's place and give me away. Do you think he will agree? And I hope you will help me to arrange the wedding. I have no idea where to start.'

Jane was delighted. 'I have not told the girls yet. They are spending a few days with my sister and their cousins so I was able to come immediately.'

Bea asked, hesitantly, 'Will Violet be very upset? She wanted Simon herself.'

'Oh, that was just a silly notion.,' Jane laughed. 'When we went to Lessing for Christmas, she became re-acquainted with a young man who had shown interest last year. I think I will be arranging another wedding before the end of this Season.'

Dora had been busy taking her things up to an attic room and remaking the bed in her room for Bea's guest. She had also set Freddie to preparing the dining room for the ladies' dinner. There would be no more cosy suppers around the kitchen table. As nice as Dora had found Mrs Hastings last year, there was a definite line between servants and family. And she made that clear to Freddie. 'No greeting his lordship like an old friend if you should meet him.'

Dora had already been put in her place. Mrs Hastings had not brought her own maid and assumed Dora would help her to dress. It was not arrogance, just the way things were done in her circle. The footman who had accompanied her had been sent back to Felixstowe with the hired cab and told to find himself a bed and return next day.

Dora also made the differing statuses clear to Bea but without revealing her own ruffled feelings. 'You are going to be a titled lady. We all have to start as we mean to go on.' Bea hugged her friend with tears in her eyes. 'Dear Dora, we may have to behave differently in public but you will always be my dearest friend.'

Bea was not looking forward to being thrust into critical high society. Her mother had been a lady and taught Bea her manners but had no personal experience to pass on. All either of them of them knew was from reading the novels they were both addicted to.

Jane reassured her with words reminiscent of John Hastings. 'Just be yourself.'

Next morning Bea went to see the Cornish's who had already been told of the embrace on the river-bank. They offered congratulations and Mr Cornish kindly ordered out his carriage to take Bea to see the Vicar to have the banns read. The vicar also showed concern for her welfare. 'This is very sudden, Miss Hastings. You are sure the gentleman really intends to marry you? You have not just been swept of your feet because he is wealthy and titled?' Bea had to show him the newspaper notice before he agreed to post the Banns.

Next, Bea went to see Mrs Potley, with instructions to close the house up until further notice. Mrs Potley fished for more information but Bea just thanked her for her service and paid her a month's wages.

Whilst Bea was out Jane had again, inadvertently, trodden on Dora's toes. She instructed Dora on which of Bea's dresses to pack saying Miss Hastings would be getting a whole new wardrobe. Dora said, Yes, ma'am,' and waited until Mrs Hastings left the room before adding two of Bea's favourite gowns and several accessories to the trunk. Mrs Hastings had also said to leave, 'That battered old bag,' behind but nothing would have persuaded Dora to relinquish charge of the old satchel of precious documents.

Bea took one look at Dora's face and asked what was wrong. 'Nothing Miss Hastings. We have just been a bit rushed.'

Bea gave Dora hug. 'Don't you dare call me Miss Hastings, or even Lady Ridgeworth when we are alone. You are, and always will be the next best thing to a mother.'

Dora wiped the tears from her eyes and gave a watery smile. 'His lordship said I was his almost mother-in-law.'

Next morning, on the train journey back to London Jane opened the topic of new clothes. With all the subtlety she could manage Bea drew Dora into the conversation and the time passed pleasantly. Discussing fashion with one's maid appeared to be quite acceptable!

Chapter 19

The next month was a whirl of activity. First and foremost, the need to dress Bea in the expected manner. She saw little of Simon and spent even less time alone with him. He had a backlog of work to catch up on, apologises to make for broken appointments and non-appearance at social events. Every stolen moment from their other activities was precious and only stoked their impatience to be married and left alone.

Simon had given Bea a ring of twisted gold with a stone as blue as his eyes. 'To remind you of me,' he said holding the ring to the side of his face. 'As if I could ever forget you,' Rea replied with a smile full of promise. Whoever it was who opened the door and saw them kissing, went quietly away.

As soon as the first of her new gowns arrived Bea was taken to afternoon teas by Jane and to a concert by Simon. She could feel everyone's curiosity like a finger on the back of her neck. Simon was a prize matrimonial catch and there were some very disappointed ladies. Although nothing was said directly to Bea, people did not always lower their voices when she was near. Hints were dropped about Simon's beautiful first wife. Why had Lord Ridgeworth chosen a widow of mediocre looks, advanced age and obscure background when there were so many lovely young ladies in Society to choose from? And why was Miss Hastings not using her married name? Bea's former marriage was known from her visit the year before although Fleming had never been mentioned by name. Hints of the marriage being too unhappy for discussion were remembered but Bea still remained an target for gossip.

Bea lived in dread of being addressed as Mrs Fleming. Their story of being romantically parted lovers held its ground but her fear never went away completely.

Simon set aside one afternoon to take Bea to meet Cynthia. She had not mentioned the child again and that scratched at Simon's conscience. In his experience ladies kept on and on about a topic they wished to discuss.

The visit was not a success. His former mother-in-law, Mrs Prentiss, was a now widow and lived in a pleasant house close to Hampstead Heath, not at all the kind of residence she had envisaged when she connived with her daughter to catch a wealthy Viscount. The Prentiss' had lived beyond their means for many years and banked on their beautiful daughter providing them with a more than just comfortable retirement.

Mrs Prentiss was not pleased to see Simon with his intended bride and did not mince her words. 'How could he replace my lovely daughter so soon?', was spoken once and silently repeated by a shake of her head every time she looked at Bea.

After requesting that Cynthia be brought down, Simon sat tight lipped while Bea tried to build a bridge that might be crossed sometime in the future. When Bea had asked about the child's education and friends, Mrs Prentiss had been quite rude. 'I trained her mother to be a lady. Cynthia will be taught all she needs to know.' Bea did not press the matter but she could not help thinking Mrs Prentiss had made a poor job of turning her daughter into a lady. Having Cynthia to live with them was not mentioned.

Meeting Cynthia was not much better. The child looked confused and even frightened when Simon approached her. She smiled tentatively at Bea but the grandmother intervened when Bea tried to get the little girl to sit next to her. Bea had never had much to do with young children but she had a feeling Cynthia was not happy. Thinking back to her own early years Bea could remember being curious about everyone and everything. By contrast Cynthia was like a little puppet who stood listlessly until her grandmother told her to say, 'Good morning' and 'Good-bye.'

'Well?' Simon asked when they left. 'I imagine my character has been thoroughly blackened judging by Cynthia's reaction.'

Bea tried to convince him that Cynthia was just shy. She felt sorry for the lonely little girl and sorry for Simon, too. There was nothing she could do now but made a resolve to bring them together somehow.

A visit Jane arranged for Bea to meet her grandmother was a resounding success.

It had been a bitter-sweet surprise when, early in the New Year, Jane had written to say Bea's grandmother wanted to meet her. The old lady was nearly blind and all her letters had to be read out to her so Jane had waited until she visited to say John's daughter had been found. In an exchange of letters Bea said she had assumed her grandmother was dead. Jane had apologised for the misunderstand. Grandmother Hastings had only been mentioned when they looked at her portrait and Bea's visit had been too short to cover every subject.

Mrs Hastings senior lived in the one of Michael's smaller properties in Surrey. They went by carriage as there was no railway station close by and they would be staying overnight.

Bea was so excited she hardly noticed the scenery as the carriage moved from the wide, clean streets of Mayfair into the dingier surrounding of South London. Once clear of the outskirts Jane said they did not have much further to go.

Bea was perched on the edge of her seat when the carriage drew up before a relatively small house set in its own grounds. She recognised it immediately from a small painting she had found hidden in her father's desk when she cleared his things. This was where Papa had grown up and he had kept the painting as the only tangible link with his childhood.

They were expected and swiftly shown up to the drawing room. Mrs Hastings senior might have been nearly blind but her hearing was acute. She was already on her feet when they entered the room. She moved confidently towards the sound of Jane's voice as she said, 'Here we are, Mama.'

'Beatrice!' the older lady sighed, holding out her hands in welcome. 'Come here dear child and kiss your Grandmama.'

Bea's grandmother was not ancient and retained signs of earlier beauty. Grey hair surrounded her smiling face and only her almost-white eyes betrayed her disability.

Bea took her hands and leaned forward to kiss her cheek. Still holding one hand Mrs Hastings towed Bea to a sofa on the far side of the sunny room. 'Let me see you,' she said. Bea was confused until her grandmother gently traced the contours of her face with shaking hands. 'Do you look like your mother? I only met her once and my sight was already fading. I wish I had been allowed to know her.'

Jane quietly left the room, unoffended that she had been forgotten.

There were so many questions and answers. So many sorrows and mysteries to be explained. Seated close together Bea did more listening than speaking and absorbed her father's background like dry earth welcomes a shower of rain.

She heard that her grandfather had forbidden any contact with his errant son. He was a neglectful husband but at the same time possessive by monitoring all his wife's correspondence and contacts. Mrs Hastings had been isolated for most of her married life but only really unhappy when her boys were sent to school. John had visited whenever he could until the fateful day that he brought his wife to be introduced. It was unfortunate that it coincided with one of her husband's infrequent visits.

'I have to say he was not overly concerned about either John's marriage or choice of wife. His main worry was what his father, the old Viscount would say.' Mr Hastings had lost no time in dragging his son and daughter-in-law up to London to be presented to the old man. Mrs Hastings shook her head sadly. 'I believe Jane has told you the outcome of that visit. His ultimatum was cruel and unjust. I only know what actually happened from my husband's account but it would have been quite in character for my father-in-law to try to control John and for my husband to follow his lead.' She paused to wipe tears from her eyes and Bea moved closer to place an arm about her grandmother's bent shoulders. 'Although it broke my heart never to see John again, I was proud of him for standing by his chosen wife. I only heard about your birth long after the event. When John died my husband said, 'Good riddance.'

Bea was shocked at such cruelty. 'I only heard about you recently,' Bea replied softly. 'Even if I had known I could not have made contact. Papa never mentioned his past and I did not know the reason for the family rift.'

Bea heard more about her father's childhood. His shyness and stammer drew contempt and his steadfast refusal to follow the tradition of selfish idleness lowered him further in the male members of the family's regard.

Oh Papa, Bea thought. *I am sorry I never understood or appreciated you enough.*

In her turn, Bea was able to tell her grandmother about her father in later life. 'He was always rather shy but I believe he was happy in his marriage and was a wonderful father to me.'

'He cared for others,' Mrs Hastings continued. 'I am thankful he had a friend who was closer than his brother. Robert was an unhappy boy.'

Bea tensed and her grandmother asked what was wrong. 'Was his name Robert Robinson Fleming?' At a nod, Bea said, 'He remained a family friend and said he owed Papa a debt he could never repay. Please continue.'

'What was I saying? Ah, yes. Robert spent his holidays with us because his father had, well, doubted his parentage. He had Robert educated and then cast him off. You say you knew him?'

Unable to help herself, Bea poured out the whole story. Mrs Hastings frowned and shook her head. 'I would never have believed that Robert could play such a cruel trick.'

'No!' Bea rushed to Rob's defence. 'It was not like that.' Her Grandmother listened, sometimes tutting, sometimes shaking her head.

'When did you find out he was married?'

'Only after he died. His wife came to see me. It was her friend, Lady Leith who put me in touch with Jane.'

They carried on, comparing memories until Mrs Hastings said they needed tea after so much talking and suddenly remembered Jane. She reached out an unerring hand and rang a small bell on the table beside her. Bea had been so focused on her grandmother she had not even looked around the room. Now she noticed that the furniture was widely spaced. Several chairs had similar small tables beside them, each with a bell. There were no un-necessary knick-knacks or hazards to prevent Mrs Hastings moving around or calling for assistance if needed.

When Jane joined them, Mrs Hastings apologised for not greeting her. Jane kissed her and said Margaret had come to take tea with them. It was a tactful way of announcing the middle-aged lady who had followed her into the room. Margaret was introduced as 'My companion and guardian angel.'

Margaret gave an impish grin and joked, 'That is why I have so many grey hairs.' Affection shone in her eyes whenever she glanced at her employer and Bea was glad to see how relaxed they were together. Margaret poured the tea carried in by a maid. She placed the saucer precariously close to the edge of the table but in the exact place Mrs Hastings expected it to be. She had a pleasant voice and a way of alerting Mrs Hastings to events beyond her range of vision without sounding as though she was giving instructions. She was always alert to her employer's needs and seemed to know when the old lady wanted something without being asked. Bea was impressed and pleased that her grandmother had such caring servants.

After they had drunk their tea, Mrs Hastings led the way out to her garden. She carried a stick but only used it to locate the top step before descending into the garden. Margaret was never far away but did not offer assistance. She did look around and gave warning of an obstacle by saying the garden boy had left his wheelbarrow by the fountain.

All the flower beds were raised to about knee height, mostly empty except those filled with fragrant herbs. Bea was told the name of each and that, later in the year, they would be joined by other sweet-smelling flowers.

Bea thought if one were blind, this would be an assessable and joyful retreat. They wandered around for a short while until the distant sound of a gong warned them it was time for dinner.

Dinner was served by the cheerful housekeeper. She named each item as it was placed, clockwise, on the old lady's plate. There was nothing that required cutting or copious gravy that could drip onto her clothing. The conversation was general and they discussed items Margaret had read out from the newspapers. 'She is a treasure,' Mrs Hastings said when Margaret suggested that Bea should be shown the scrapbook when they returned to the drawing room.

The book was bulky with more tangible items than printed words. The few pictures were identified by buttons or ribbons stuck down beside them. It was a masterpiece. The newspaper cutting of her father's death had a page to itself, surrounded by a folded paper frame.

Time was forgotten until Jane gave a soft yawn. Margaret had lit a lamp for the visitors' benefit but no-one had been in any hurry to go to bed as they talked. Mrs Hastings finally said she must not keep them from their beds any longer. 'I have enjoyed today and hope we may spend more time together on another occasion.' She reached for Bea's hand and smiled. 'I am so looking forward to your wedding. Please will you invite Lady Leith, I would enjoy meeting her again after such a long separation.'

Bea kissed her grandmother goodnight and followed her up the stairs.

Bea thought her grandmother a remarkable woman. She had started planning her own life as soon as her husband died. She had set the rules about placement of furniture, etcetera, so she could remain independent. One hardly noticed that she could not see very much beyond blurred movements. It would be a wrench to leave her next day.

Bea went to bed but did not try to sleep. She had a lot to think about. Rob's devotion to John Hastings was easily explained. While the other boys all had a generous allowance, Robert had worked at any odd jobs available to pay his own way. He was too proud to sponge off his friend. Even when he joined John for holidays, he had found ways of making himself useful.

They had been separated when John went to university but still kept in touch. Rob had married a lady with a large dowry and set himself up in business. After such a hard start in life Bea could understand why he made a point of enjoying his success. Bea did not think it so praiseworthy that he had been unfaithful to his wife. And with his resourcefulness, surely, he could have come up with some scheme other than a bogus marriage to protect her independence. Yet, even knowing the negative side of Rob's life, Bea could not help but be grateful for his support and even his version of loving care.

Thinking of all the other things she had learned today was too much for her tired brain and Bea fell asleep before she had even started on another topic.

Bea had had expected her grandmother to take breakfast in her room but the old lady got up in time to join her guests at the table. 'I may laze about every other day,' she insisted. 'I will not waste of moment of your visit.'

When it was time to say goodbye, they hugged and kissed and prolonged the parting as long as they could.

As she said goodbye, Bea thanked Margaret for her devoted care. 'Don't you worry, Miss Hastings,' Margaret replied. 'I will never be far from her side. Perhaps attending your wedding will encourage her to get out and about more often.'

Bea mentioned this to Jane on their ride home. 'Mama can travel when necessary but she hates it when strangers tried to fuss other her. Margaret will keep them at bay,' Jane laughed.

Bea thought of all her family had missed through the spite of others. Her Papa especially. Had he written to his mother and thought his letters ignored?

Bea had not consciously missed having a family. She had been loved, taught and cared for by her parents and given enough freedom to form her own opinions. Meeting the Hastings filled a gap she had not known was there and Simon's descriptions of his own family made her eager to meet them too.

Chapter 20

A few days later Simon arranged to take Bea to see his solicitor. 'Under normal circumstances the settlement would be dealt with by your father or, possibly, an uncle. Lessing is too young and you are more than capable of managing your own affairs.' Bea thanked him for the compliment. Very few people considered a woman's intelligence worth praising. Simon went on, 'You will have a generous allowance and I must repay Mrs Hastings for your new clothes.'

'I paid for those myself,' Bea said indignantly.

Simon smiled. 'Then your savings must be sadly depleted.'

'I am not a pauper! You will still be getting a substantial dowry.'

'I am not marrying you for your money,' Simon said and kissed her. His attempt at a leering expression held far too much tenderness to be effective. They were in the small sitting room Jane allowed them to use for their private moments and the money was forgotten for a while.

Footsteps beyond the door reminded them that privacy was more of an illusion and drew apart. Simon loosened his cravat and returned to the conversation. What Bea considered substantial would hardly compare to his own wealth.

'Then you shall keep it for your own use.'

'You might want to reconsider that when you find out how much it is. And it will all become yours anyway. I am sure you will not fritter it all away. But it is the law.'

'Not necessarily. The law does not actually forbid a woman having assets. If I gift it back to you, it will be personal property, like jewellery or artworks.' The irony made Bea smile. Rob had done much the same. But she would not mention that.

Simon misinterpreted the smile. 'You want me to have it? Most women resent giving everything into their husband's hands.' He knew of several ladies who owned property. Bea's assets were hardly worth arguing about. The shop had been leased and any money raised from sale of the stock would not last long once Bea had to keep up with London fashioned.

Thinking aloud he continued. 'Technically a wife's assets become part of her husband's estate. He can do whatever he likes with them. I will give them back to you.'

Bea thought he was being a bit condescending. Not intentionally but she could see he was not taking her seriously. She could not stop him taking control of her assets but his offer warmed her heart. 'Wait until you see what is involved,' Bea cautioned.

Simon rubbed his hands together in the way Mr Dicken's had described Scrooge. 'Perhaps you ought to let me see your fortune before we go.'

Bea fetched the satchel and tipped the contents out onto a table. Simon's eyes widened as the picked them up, one after the other and estimated their worth.

'How? He asked incredulously.

My mother invested under Rob's advice. And I have added to it.'

'He knew? He married you under false pretences and left all this in your name?

'He was not all bad,' Bea insisted.' I know you don't want to hear any good about him but he did it to keep me safe.' Bea could not divulge all her grandmother had told her about Rob. At least, not yet.

Her defence of Fleming ought to have made him angry. He did not like to think of her time with Fleming but knowledge changed opinions. 'We will have to get expert advice. Whatever the case may be, I promise you will always have a say in what happens to all this.' He tapped the papers and Bea threw herself into his arms.

As expected, the solicitor was amazed and disapproving of Simon's intentions. His belief that ladies were incapable of managing financial affairs was turned on its head by the evidence before him. In the last few years Bea had made several profitable investments to add to her inheritance. He said he would need to look into the matter further before leaving them to consult a colleague.

'It doesn't matter,' Bea said. 'Let things be done as usual.'

Simon was humbled by her trust and his voice was hoarse as he promised she would never regret it. He was about to seal his vow with a kiss when the lawyer returned.

'My colleague has suggested a compromise. Miss Hastings, when she becomes Viscountess Ridgewood, may retain possession of the house at Little Moorings and have a generous allowance.' He did not report that it was in the hope of his Lordship coming to his senses after the first euphoria of marriage had worn off. 'Once you are married, we will be able to discuss the matter again.'

Simon was dis-satisfied. He resented the fussy concession and saw through the lawyer's evasion. 'We most certainly will,' he insisted before saying their business was finished for the moment and guided Bea from the room.

'Who is he to say what we may or may not do?' Simon complained as the carriage took them back to Jane's house. Bea snuggled closer to his side, more in love with her noble lord than she had thought possible.

There was just one more matter to clear up. They were going through the guest list with Jane when Simon spotted Lady Leith's name.

'You know Lady Leith?'

Somehow the question of when Bea had discovered her marriage was false had never come up before.

'When Rob died his widow came to see me, accompanied by Lady Leith. It was Lady Leith who put me in touch with Jane. She is a long-time friend of my grandmother.'

'So, she knows all the details?' Simon asked worriedly. He was not acquainted with the lady but knew of her by reputation. She did not seem the kind of person who would share her dangerous knowledge. And Mrs Robinson Fleming was even more unlikely to want the story to get out. 'Who else knows?'

'Lady Leith was very discreet when she contacted me,' Jane assured him. 'Nothing was put in writing and she only said Bea was in trouble before she was sure I had Bea's best interests at heart.'

Simon relaxed. Bea had not continued her relationship with Fleming knowing the marriage was false. He had reluctantly assumed she had done it in self-defence but knowing her true innocence warmed him.

Bea's secret was safe. Nothing could mar their future happiness.

153

Chapter 21

Bea's assumed widowhood made it inappropriate for her to wear a white dress and veil for her wedding. In consultation with Jane and the dressmaker she settled for a gown of heavy satin in a shade richer than cream but not quite pink. The wide skirt felt cumbersome as she had never worn a crinoline before and she had to remember to take small steps or the skirt bobbed up and down like a boat in a storm.

On her wedding morning, Bea looked at her reflection in the long mirror. Her hair had been swept up in a mass of small coils, partially hidden by a jaunty hat of the same material as her gown. Instead of a bouquet she had a corsage of rosemary and pink rosebuds pinned to her bodice by her mother's gold bar brooch.

'Beautiful,' Jane said, looking over Bea's shoulder and Bea almost believed it. She had heard it said that all brides were beautiful on their wedding day. Perhaps it was some kind of magic but she certainly looked better than usual.

Excited young voices announced the arrival of her attendants. Violet looked ravishing in an elaborate blue gown and Bea accepted that, bride or not, she would be put in the shade. Simon's cousin, Iris, was also a rival for the limelight. Her beauty was enhanced by innocence and a lack of vanity. Lily was just so full of excitement she was sure to draw attention.

Hey Ho, Bea thought. *Simon thinks I am beautiful and that is all that matters.*

Jane ushered the girls from the room and gave Bea one last kiss before following them. Only Dora remained. She was dewy eyed but had stayed firmly in her role of maid during the preparations. Now she took Bea by the shoulders and looked into her eyes. 'Your parents would be proud of you and it breaks my heart that they cannot be with you today., Her breath caught in a small sob. 'By happy, my lovely girl.' She kissed Bea's cheek and hurried from the room.

Bea was having trouble suppressing her own tears. Dora deserved a more prominent place. She had been almost a mother, a trusted advisor and the best friend Bea had, or was ever likely to have.

Michael came to the door to say it was time for them to leave. He looked so uneasy Bea forgot her own fluttering nerves. She even laughed when he managed to say she looked nice.

Bea and Simon were to be married at St George's Church on Hanover square. The usual crowd of onlookers gathered around the gates had assessed the quality of the arriving guests and only the most cynical were disappointed in the bride. Dora was waiting in the porch with the girls. She gave Bea's gown and unnecessary tweak and hurried into her place. Against her wishes Dora was to sit with Mrs Armitage near the front of the church. Simon had asked it as a favour as Mrs Armitage never went into society and would need support.

It had taken a letter from Bea to get Maria Armitage there at all. *As a favour,* she had written. *Simon's family will not be complete without you.*

'Ready?' Bea asked Michael and the girls. 'Then let's go.'

Michael looked into the church and froze. Violet poked him in the back and hissed, 'Get a move on, Mickie.' He had been trying to shed the childish name and Violet's use of it now made him forget his nervousness. He turned to snap at his sister but Bea grabbed his arm and almost dragged him into the church.

The pews were not crowded but it was a sizeable congregation. Every invitation had been accepted. Lords, ladies, politicians and civic dignitaries with their wives, had jostled for the best view and all turned as the organ heralded Bea's arrival.

Bea saw none of them. Her eyes were focused on Simon. His smile was like a magnet and she could not control her feet as she almost ran towards him. Simon took her hand and raised it to his lips. There were murmurs from the congregation but Bea did not hear them either Michael was still clinging to her other arm and she had to shake him loose.

Rev Armitage, who had been allowed to conduct the service, whispered, 'Let go of her hand' and Simon replied, 'Never.' A tall man on Simon's far side gave a bark of laughter.

The service passed in a blur. Bea had an anxious moment when the vicar asked if there was any known reason why they should not be joined in matrimony but no-one called out to condemn her. She repeated her vows quietly but clearly and Simon slid the ring of twisted gold onto her finger. They were proclaimed man and wife. Simon kissed her lips and a sigh went up from the ladies behind them.

The rest of the service dragged. It was high church and included communion and a sermon. It was only as Bea signed her name in the register that she compared it to her other marriage. She pushed the thought aside. This was real. Not a sham to be hidden away in a cold office. Simon loved her and wanted the world to know it.

On their way back down the aisle, Bea noticed Jane, her grandmother and Margaret in the front pew. All the family she had. She stopped and broke a sprig of rosemary from her corsage. 'For your memory book, grandmama,' she whispered and kissed the rather damp cheek. On the other side of the aisle, Rev Armitage had joined his wife and a fierce looking lady who glared at Bea as she passed. Bea turned her head away and did not think of her again until later. She remembered to acknowledge the sea of smiling faces but was only really aware of Simon's hand covering hers on his coat sleeve.

The outdoor crowd cheered as they left the church but it was not over yet. They had to stand while the congregation flooded out to shower them with dried petals as they ran to the open, flower and ribbon decorated carriage.

As the carriage moved away, Simon said, 'Hello, Lady Ridgeworth' and kissed her to the cheers of the crowd.

The reception was a near nightmare for Bea. Every time she was introduced, she expected to be recognised. Gradually it eased as people she knew crowded around her. She had met Rev and Mrs Armitage the night before when they brought Iris to stay with Jane. Lady Leith spoke briefly before giving way to the fierce little lady who had glared at her. 'My mother' Simon told her, stiff with anger when his mother merely sniffed as though she had detected an unpleasant smell. The handsome man who had been Simon's best man was introduced as Lord Truro who slapped Simon on the back and stole a quick kiss from Bea. 'I wish I'd seen her first,' he laughed when Simon pulled him away.

With so many guests the wedding breakfast was served as a buffet but Bea did not get to taste any of it. She found her grandmother seated with Lady Leith and Margaret. Margaret gave up her chair to Bea and stood behind the old lady.

'Thank you for coming, Lady Leith. I wanted to thank you for making me known to my family but did not know your direction. 'No thanks needed, my dear.' Lady Leith replied and touched her friend's arm. 'You have brought me back to Agnes. That is thanks enough.'

Simon's mother thrust herself between them and addressed Lady Leith. 'You might have offered to bring me as we are neighbours. The hired carriage was most uncomfortable.'

'I came by train Matilda. You would not have enjoyed that, mixing with the hoi-palloi.'

'Enough of that here!' Lady Ridgeworth said just as Simon came up to join them. 'Mother!' he said sternly but she ignored him too and stalked away.

Simon started to say something but Lady Leith shook her head. 'Matilda will never change. Named for an empress and tries to behave like one.' She gave them a cheeky grin. 'We made our come-out together and she has never forgiven me for out-ranking her. Both before and after we married.'

Simon took Bea's arm and led her away to a quiet corner. Bea placed a finger on his lips before he could speak. 'No. You cannot apologise for other people. But do not worry, I will not meet rudeness with rudeness.'

'I love you,' he whispered.

When it was time to cut the cake, Michael forgot the speech he had been practising and spoke from the heart. Bea nearly cried when he said it was an honour to stand in for the uncle he had never known.

Simon's reply was equally short, reaffirming the story they had concocted. 'It has made my life complete to claim her at last.'

With their duty done, Simon told Bea to go and change. 'We have to leave soon.'

It could not be soon enough for Bea. It was a relief to leave the crowd and seek the sanctuary of her bedroom. Dora had everything ready and Bea was soon back to another round of kisses and farewells.

'Where are we going? Bea asked as the carriage drew away. Simon had been very secretive about the honeymoon. He grinned at her now. 'Cornwall. You said you wanted to see the ocean.'

The journey was too long to complete that day and Simon wanted their first night together to be in one of his own properties. 'We won't get there today. I have a small house on the Hampshire border. They will be expecting us.' He drew her close and Bea raised her face for a kiss that had to be brief as they had already reached the station.

Bea was surprised to see Dora. She had forgotten all else than finally being alone with Simon. Beside Dora was a tall, serious looking man Simon introduced as his valet, Noakes. Dora carried a basket that she handed to Bea when they found their seats. 'Something to keep you going. I don't suppose you ate much at the reception.'

'That was thoughtful,' Simon remarked trying to peak into the basket. He grinned. 'A man needs to keep his strength up!'

Bea giggled. 'Do you know what your nephew said to me as we were leaving?' Simon shook his head. 'He said he did not want to be a Viscount and he was relying on me to save him.'

This train had no private compartments and other people were taking their seats so Simon could only chuckle and say, 'The cheeky beggar.'

Bea was glad to have the picnic but refused the lemonade. She did not know how long it would be before she could relieve herself. No-one tried to engage them in conversation but they received some indulgent looks. Bea blushed. Was it so obvious they were newly-weds?

Simon's property was a pretty little house, smaller than the one at Little Moorings. A pleasant faced woman, welcomed them and said a meal would be ready whenever they wanted it. 'Thank you. I will just go and wash my hands,' Bea said before Simon had a chance. She had been aching to become Simon's wife in all ways but now the moment was here, she felt suddenly shy.

Dora, Noakes and their luggage had not yet arrived so the housekeeper showed Bea up to their room. Bea slipped behind the vanity screen with relief. She hadn't been able to explain her sudden departure to Simon. The bodily needs they had been thinking about for a whole month could be hinted at but the need to pass water seemed far to0 private. How long did it take for a couple to feel easy about basic functions?

Simon was thinking along similar lines. He had drunk most of the lemonade.

Neither of them took very long and Bea tiptoed down to the tiny parlour as though she was doing something very naughty. The twinkle in Simon's eyes told her his thoughts were definitely naughty although he kept his greeting to a swift kiss before seating her at the table. Bea was not sure what they ate. The naughty thoughts kept her tongue-tied but her frequent blushes gave her away.

Simon pushed away his plate. 'Have you eaten enough?' he asked hopefully. 'Dora will have your things laid out now so why don't you go up. I will be with you soon.'

Dora was being a perfect maid. She had washing water and towels behind the screen and did not try to chat as Bea undressed. She had felt that way once and prayed Bea's happiness would not be so short-lived. The nightgown Jane had chosen was of sheer, pink silk that slid smoothly over Bea's body when she moved. Dora dowsed all but one lamp and murmured, 'God Bless, love,' as she left the room.

Bea did not know what to do. Was she supposed to get into the bed she had avoided looking at? Should she put on a more substantial wrapper?

Simon had been waiting close to his door and sighed with relieve when he heard Dora pass. He had been celibate for nearly six years and the woman of his dreams was in the next room. He felt ready to explode. *Take your time,* he repeated like a mantra. *Go slowly, Bea is a virgin. Don't frighten her.*

He tapped softly on her door and went in. Bea was standing on the far side of the room in the most seductive garment he had ever seen. It covered her from neck to ankles but the lamp behind her outlined every line of her body. She gave him a shy smile and he was lost. In a few quick steps he had her in his arms. His resolve to go slowly evaporated under the heat of Bea's innocent response. Her gown slid to the floor. His banyan followed and they were wrapped in each other's arms on the bed.

'I did not mean to be so rough,' Simon confessed sometime later. 'Did I hurt you?'

Bea smiled up at him dreamily. 'I think you took me to heaven. Is it always like this?'

'No. I have never felt like this before. I never, well, touched Monica but in my younger days….'

Bea placed a finger against his lips. 'You are a man. I understand.' She frowned, 'Well actually I don't. I knew what was to happen but I have never wanted to do that with anyone else.'

Simon flopped back on his pillows laughing. 'Oh, Bea. You never cease to surprise me. I don't think it is normal to discuss past experience on one's wedding night. And certainly not with a new wife.'

Bea rolled until she half covered him. Her hair tickled his chest. He could feel himself responding as Bea asked, 'What do people talk about after making love?'

Simon rolled until she was beneath him again. 'They don't talk.' His hand slid down to her groin and gently probed. 'They are too busy.'

Chapter 22

It was late when Bea woke up. The place beside her was cold and empty. She sat up with a jerk and called, 'Simon!'

It was Dora who came through from the tiny washing area. 'His lordship said not to disturb you. I have water ready on a spirit stove for your tea.'

Tea! Bea fell back against the pillows with a quiet chuckle. Sometime during the night Simon had opened a bottle of champagne. She hadn't liked the taste very much but it made her bold and she had mimicked some of Simon's actions until he growled and loved her again. She tucked the sheet under her arms, shy of Dora seeing her nakedness.

A long, warm bath eased some of the soreness in places Bea had not known could be so sensitive. Dora carried out her duties with the minimum of fuss and hardly spoke until Bea was dressed for the day.

'Are you back to earth enough to talk?' Dora asked.

Bea nodded, reluctant to let go of her lingering euphoria.

'His Lordship went out for a walk and left a note I will bring up with your breakfast tray. The housekeeper, Mrs Adams, is very fond of Lord Ridgeworth and would sing his praises all day if I had time to listen.' Dora snorted. 'Not like that valet. I never met a more tight-lipped fellow. But efficient.' She added grudgingly. 'Hardly said a word that was not to do with luggage or where to sit on the train. I'll go and get your tray.'

Bea thought it rather silly to have breakfast brought up when she was already dressed. Was this to be a new habit? She hoped not as she would rather eat breakfast with Simon. She wished she knew more about his habits and usual routine. A little of it was explained in the note he had left. It began, 'My Darling wife,' and said he was an early riser but would see her very soon.' The last two words were underlined. Bea could hardly wait.

Dora stood over her until she had drunk another cup of tea and eaten a small piece of toast before allowing her to go in search of Simon.

Bea did not have to search. The house only had two down-stairs rooms and Simon was pacing the carpet in the parlour until he heard Bea coming down the stairs. Dora was following so he just took Bea's hands and dropped a quick kiss on her cheek. 'Do you feel up to a walk? It is warm enough not to need a coat.'

The garden was tiny and Simon opened the gate so they could stroll down the lane, away from the village. 'Do you come here often?' Bea asked.

Simon shook his head. He could not tell her it had been his retreat, an escape from Town and the constant gossip about Monica. Instead he told her about Ridgeworth Court, the ancestral home in Surrey. And other houses dotted around the country. Bea thought it wasteful but did not want to say anything that sounded critical. Simon was indulgent but he had his own way of life, they could not live in this blissful bubble for ever.

They spent a quiet day and planned to continue they journey to Cornwall tomorrow. It would mean an early start and his eyes sparkled when he added, 'And early night.' What with all the recent excitement, travelling and an almost sleepless night, the loving was gentle and they fell asleep in each other's arms.

The train journey to Cornwall took most of the day. They filled it by talking about the wedding, their likes and dislikes and general background things there had been no time to explore before. Their lives had been so different. While Bea had never gone far from Cambridge, Simon had travelled widely, even as far as Italy. Bea's life had been simple while Simon had, from a very young age, been surrounded by pomp and formality. They were both going to have to make adjustments.

It was evening by the time they reached Lord Truro's home. They were to stay in the dower-house in the grounds but far enough away from main house to give them privacy. Truro's staff had everything prepared and would come daily but only Dora and Noakes would stay there overnight.

Next morning Bea asked, 'Where is the sea?'

'We are not on the coast but we can visit now if you wish.'

Simon drove the small open carriage with Bea tucked up close beside him. Within minutes there was a subtle change in the light and a glinting blue line on the horizon. A narrow lane led down to a sandy cove with only a few fishermen's huts. No-one was about so Simon tied the horse in the shade and left it with a bucket of water saying the rough grass would be salty.

Bea looked at the gently rolling water. Rocky outcrops on either side restricted the view and the water was not as dramatic as she expected of an ocean. The North Sea, seen from the harbour in Felixstowe, was rougher than this.

'Would you like to swim? I would enjoy teaching you.'

I don't have a bathing dress. And where would I change?'

Simon grinned. 'There is a lake at Ridgeworth. I can arrange for everyone to avoid the area and you won't need a bathing costume.' It sounded deliciously wicked. For today Bea had to be content with taking off her shoes and stockings and babbling her feet in the cold water. She was not wearing a crinoline but all her new dresses had wide skirts and several petticoats which she had to hold up in a bundle so as not to get them wet. 'In a day to two I will take you to see the real ocean,' Simon promised. It would mean another fairly long journey and an overnight stay but for the moment they were happy just to be together.

The next day they walked up to the main house. An imposing mansion with a park and formal gardens. Bea was surprised that Simon intended them to go inside and look around. It sounded very intrusive, looking around someone's home when they were not there. Simon assured her it was not uncommon for people, of the right sort, to visit the grand houses of the nobility. Not the private rooms, just the state apartments and gardens.

Simon had spent holidays here with Alan and his family and was greeted warmly. Simon declined the housekeeper's escort and showed Bea around himself. It was very grand. In the portrait gallery she stood before a painting of the marquis with his young wife and two very young children. They looked so happy that Bea was saddened to hear Lady Truro had died before her daughter was one year old.

It reminded Bea of Cynthia. Their visit had not been a success. The only other time Bea had mentioned the chid, Simon had said there was plenty of time and changed the subject. It would have to be addressed at some point but not now.

On the day of Bea's promised visit to see the ocean she could hardly sit still. There was no railway close by so Simon hired a small carriage he could drive himself. The roads were narrow with very little traffic. Sometimes there was a glimpse of the sea and at others, high banks turned the road almost into a tunnel. 'Are we nearly there yet?' she kept asking and Simon laughingly said she was too impatient.

They were to stay in a small hotel and had left Dora and Noakes behind in an attempt to appear merely genteel. This was a time for them alone without the formality their lives would assume once they returned to London. Bea wanted to see the ocean but Simon insisted on having lunch before taking her to the viewing spot. Bea's excitement amused him and he was happy to let it build.

They walked along a rough path to the very tip of England. 'Land's End,' Simon announced like a conjuror pulling a rabbit from a hat.

Bea clung onto his arm as they neared the edge of the cliffs. One thing she really did not like was heights but she forgot that at the magnificence all around her. He coaxed her forward until she could look down. Even on this bright Spring day huge waves crashed against the rocks far below. The spray caught the sunlight to create dancing rainbows. After a few moments they retreated to a safe distance so Bea could look around. On three sides there was nothing but water, heaving and sighing like a mighty sleeping beast. 'Your ocean, my lady. Three thousand miles out there is America. To your left and a little behind is the Continent and over there,' he swung her round to the right, 'is Ireland and Wales. Bea was too overwhelmed to reply. Simon watched her face and thought Bea's radiant expression beat the view, hands down.

When she had looked her fill, they sat on the rough grass, not talking, hardly touching until Simon gently eased her down onto her back. Bea closed her eyes as the sun burned her eyelids. The shadow of Simon's descending head made her open them to look into his eyes and they kissed. Aware that they were too exposed to take things any further Simon pulled Bea to her feet and allowed her one last look around. The western sun was low in the sky and gleamed across the water like a shining highway to heaven. Dazed by the beauty Bea was reluctant to leave. 'I will never forget this day,' she said as they ambled back to the hotel.

A group of artists who were also staying at the hotel had returned before them and taken up residence the bar-cum-lounge. They looked up and cheerfully re-shuffled their seats to make room for the newcomers.

It would have appeared rude to go straight past them and up their room. 'What will you have, Mr Armitage? And your lady?' the owner called from behind the bar.

Simon ordered ale for himself and cordial for Bea. In the short time it took to get the drinks the landlord had also introduced the other guests. Mr and Mrs Stowell were from Nottingham and the younger man was their son. The other older man was a local simply called Amos, an artist from Bude. Bea took the seat beside Mrs Stowell and said her name. The lady laughed. 'What a co-incidence! My second name is Beatrice. Mary Beatrice Oakley, as was.'

Soon they were all chatting about the day's activities. The artists' opened their folders and Bea fell in love with a small watercolour painted from the Land's End headland. Simon asked if he might buy it. 'It's not really finished,' Amos told him. 'It needs some more definition.'

'Oh, please don't change it. That slightly blurred atmosphere is just as I will remember the view. Memories are never quite so …' Beas couldn't think of the right words.

Mrs Stowell smiled indulgently. 'I think you mean emotion adds colours that were not really there. Or,' she looked from Bea to Simon and back, 'perhaps the emotions blur the image. I can see you have had a lovely day.'

Bea blushed. Was it so obvious that they were on their honeymoon?

No-one made any suggestion of changing for dinner so Bea just went upstairs to tidy herself. The meal was served at a long, wooden table. Dishes were placed in the centre and passed around for everyone to help themselves. Ale and cordial came in jugs. Everyone talked but no-one asked probing questions. It was a pleasant evening to end a lovely day.

'I thought we would never get away,' Simon said as they climbed the stairs. He placed the picture on the chest of drawers and promised to have it framed. 'I never gave you a wedding gift. All I could think of was this.'

This was a long, slow loving. The perfect end to a perfect day.

They were late rising next morning, adding one last memory to this time out of time.

Only the hotel owner was about as they left. He had wrapped Bea's precious painting and tied it with string so Bea could carry it easily. As plain Mr Armitage Simon carried their bags to the hired carriage.

Bea sat close to Simon trying to convince herself this was not an ending. They had not given a definite date for their return to London and planned to stay several more days before making a leisurely journey home. But she could not shake the feeling that things would never be the same again.

Chapter 23

Bea went straight upstairs when they reached the dower house. Travelling always seemed to make it urgent to get to the necessary.

Simon was detained by Noakes who handed him a telegram. He frowned as he ripped it open, very few people knew where they were. He closed his eyes after reading the short message. *Dear God! How was he going to tell Bea?*

Bea knew there was something wrong as soon as Simon walked into the bedroom. He took her in his arms and just held her. She could feel his heart thumping under her ear but it was not passion.

Bea eased back. 'Simon?' He shook his head sadly and handed her a crumpled piece of paper. Bea smoothed it out and read the words: THE NEWS IS OUT.JANE.

It could only mean one thing. If Simon had not been holding her Bea would have fallen to the ground. 'Oh, what have I done?' she groaned just as Simon was saying sorry. Each was thinking of the other. They spoke together, 'I should never have agreed to marry you. My selfishness has involved you in a scandal.' 'I have let you down. I promised to keep you safe'.

Simon tilted Bea's chin so she had to look at him. 'Once and for Always. We will face this together. You were innocent and I will swear it in a court of law if necessary. We must get back to town as soon as possible.'

'Nooooo!' Bea wailed. 'I can't go back.'

'Yes, you can. You have too much courage to allow gossips to ruin our marriage.'

Simon left Bea sitting on the side of the bed and went to find Noakes. It was too late to leave today but Noakes must arrange for them to get back to town as soon as possible. As Noakes turned away Simon caught his arm. 'Whatever you may hear, Bea is my wife and will stay my wife. I have not told you everything so you must trust me. I will explain but not now.'

When Simon returned to the bedroom Bea was coiled up on the bed crying. Dora stood helplessly by her side with tears running down her cheeks. When Simon sent her an enquiring glance, she just shook her head and left the room.

Simon gathered Bea close. To ask what was wrong was pointless. He could not even promise everything would be alright. They would survive but at what cost?

Bea looked at him in despair and whispered, 'My courses have started,' before burying her face in his jacket again.

Cruel, cruel fate. He could not even comfort her with the ultimate gift of his loving. All he could do was hold her until Dora came to made Bea ready for bed.

He paced back and forth in the parlour until Dora came down stairs carrying a bundle of laundry. She barred his way to the stairs but her expression and voice were sympathetic when she spoke. 'My lord, I have given Bea a soothing draught. It will help her to sleep. I cannot forbid you to go to her but, please…..' Dora pursed her lips knowing she was on the brink of impertinence.

'I know.' Simon replied sadly. 'If I sit with her now, will you have your meal and come back later? Bea needs you more than she needs me at the moment.' His little speech raised him in Dora's estimation. It was a rare man who put a woman's needs above his own.

The journey next day was a bitter contrast to the excitement of only a few days before. Even the weather had turned against them. The blue skies were replaced by a dull grey blanket of cloud that soon turned to rain that added to the gloomy atmosphere. They hardly spoke as Simon had run out of comforting words and Bea knew he did not want to hear her taking the blame on her own shoulders. Bea dozed from time to time, still under the influence of the painkilling mixture Dora had almost forced down her throat.

With Bea suffering physical as well as mental distress, Simon insisted on breaking their journey at Salisbury. Bea was put straight to bed in one of the best rooms the station hotel had to offer. Dora stayed with her and Simon spent a lonely and uncomfortable night in the tiny room and lumpy bed provided for servants.

By next morning Bea was feeling a little better, at least bodily. The griping pain in her belly had lessened to become a dull ache that spread throughout her body until she felt too heavy to move. 'It has never been so bad before,' she said to Dora as she got dressed.

Grace Hastings had made sure her daughter was prepared well in advance of puberty. In her own lonely childhood Grace had thought she was about to die at the first show of blood. Her only knowledge came from old books, all written by men, and almost incomprehensible. Common sense was more useful than exact information so she had just told Bea it was quite natural and nature's way of preparing her to be a mother. It was a little uncomfortable and inconvenient for a few days but nothing to worry about.

Dora, even less informed, was more intuitive. 'I think your body is confused. All the excitement of the wedding, the new experiences and then a shock made you too tense. And all this travel is not helping.'

As the train rattled its way eastwards Bea's dread grew. How would they be received? This was not just her scandal. It would affect Simon and her family. Even Simon's when the story reached Gloucestershire, as it was bound to do. Yesterday, in her clear-minded moments she had told Simon she would go away but he would not hear of it. 'I love you, Bea. Once and for Always. I will settle for nothing less. We will see this through together.'

Bea would have been less worried if she were alone. She could disappear again but that would not stop others being hurt. She remembered her father saying, 'Life is not always easy.' With her recently acquired knowledge Bea appreciated that he had learned that the hard way. Her parents had suffered because they wanted to be together. She wanted to be with Simon but she did not want him hurt. Bea's thoughts went around in circles, always coming back to the same point. They had promised to love each other for better or worse. Now it was time to put that love to the test.

No definite date had been set for their return but they had decided on an excuse for cutting their honeymoon short. Bea did not have to pretend as she carried out his instructions. Simon's staff took one look at their new mistress's wan face and drooping posture and feared the worst. On her introductory visit before the marriage she had been bright and friendly. Now she looked too ashamed to face them. Bea was too distressed to notice the wooden greetings but Simon frowned and took Bea up to her bedroom himself. Thank goodness she had Dora to act as a buffer.

'Go to bed,' Simon whispered as he kissed her cheek. 'I have some letters to write but will return shortly.' He went to his study and found the London papers laid out on his desk. They were not as pristine as he usually received them and knew that they had been passed around in his absence. He deliberately left them where them where they were and rang for the butler.

'Lady Ridgeworth was taken ill several days ago. She insists she is feeling better but I want a reliable doctor to check. I know you are all concerned and trust you will keep the house quiet so she can rest. Mrs Cotton will inform the kitchens when my wife feels like eating again.' He had done all he could to lead speculation away from the scandal.

Simon then dashed off a note to Jane saying he would call on her in the morning.

Jane arrived on their doorstep before Simon had finished his breakfast. 'How is she? 'Jane asked anxiously.

'Terribly upset for the trouble she has caused us. Her words not mine.'

'Or mine!' Jane replied staunchly.

There was another knock on the door and Michael came in with Freddie. Freddie had a black eye.

Jane shook her head. 'I told him brawling in the street would not make matters any better. Simon, what are we going to do?'

'Nothing without Bea's consent. I'll go up and fetch her now.'

Bea was already on her way down and met Simon before he could climb the stairs. She had heard arrivals and could not let Simon face them alone. Dora came one step behind.

'You, too, Dora,' Simon added as he led Bea towards the drawing room. 'Mrs Hastings and Lessing are already here with Freddie who has a black eye. As I have told Bea repeatedly, we are all in this together Noakes will be down in a moment.'

Simon had taken Noakes aside before they left the Cornish hotel to tell him the contents of the telegram. 'We must go back to town immediately on the pretext that Lady Ridgeworth has been ill.' The staff would get nothing out of his loyal valet.

They held a Council of War. If the staff were surprised at the inclusion of a maid and footman, they were astonished when Noakes joined them.

Simon explained Noakes presence to the others. 'Noakes is totally trustworthy and has a wise head on his shoulders.'

Noakes was given all the facts which were also new to Michael and Freddie. All three were outraged and showed it in different way. Simon hushed them and asked, 'Have you any suggestions, Noakes?'

Noakes was silent for so long Simon thought he was going to refuse to answer. Finally, he looked around cleared his throat and bowed to Bea, placing himself firmly on her side.

'My lady, I have read the papers. As yet nothing has been printed that can be challenged. Gossip is hard to trace. I suggest we behave as though it has nothing to do with us.'

They went through the papers together, making a note of all the innuendoes and discounting them. The newspaper editors had been very clever. There were clues to identity but no names. They wanted to sell their papers without leaving themselves open to charges. It was always easy to direct any blame at a female, especially one unknown to society. Bea was the obvious target and Simon wrote down the main points raised.

a.   The woman concerned was a bigamist.

b.   She had beguiled a noble lord into an affair while still under the protection of an unnamed man only referred to as Mr F. and trapped him into marriage.

c.   She had heartlessly involved her innocent relations.

A second list was made refuting all the claims.

First and foremost, Bea was not a bigamist as she had not previous marriage.

She had not consorted with Simon during her relationship with Fleming.

They were both well known in their own sphere and someone would surely have noticed if they had been meeting.

Simon had known of the liaison before asking Bea to marry him.

Jane had known of Bea's bogus marriage to Fleming before inviting Bea into her home.

In short, Bea was innocent of all charges. It was not much to go on.

How to disprove the allegations without admitting they contained a grain of distorted truth had them at a standstill. Noakes' final advice was the same as his first. Everyone concerned would act as though the matter had nothing to do with them.

That was not going to be easy. Bea had an honest, open nature. Simon had laughingly told her she would never make a gambler as she could not conceal her emotions. The others were more practised in keeping a bland expression on their faces whatever their thoughts might be.

The meeting broke up with all but Bea going about their everyday business. Left alone her brain whirled with confusion. How had the news got out? Very few people knew the facts and she had believed them all to be trustworthy. A trust that they were putting into practice now, risking their own reputations by supporting her now. It was a disaster and Bea could not see any hopeful outcome.

Bea picked up Simon's lists and picked holes in the conclusions. How were Simon and Jane supposed to have known about the marriage if they had not been in contact? The story of meeting, loving and being kept apart did not explain how they had suddenly come together when they were both free. The obvious answer was correspondence. Letters could have been going backwards and forwards over many years. It still smacked of deceit while Simon and Bea were both in marriages but it was a much lesser crime than meeting.

To have been in correspondence with Jane was also open to question. If it was innocent, why had she not shared the news with her family?

Bea's head was aching with the worry and she kept coming back to her weakness in leaving the anonymity of life alone for the joy of being with Simon. No matter how many times he said it was not her fault, Bea was still wracked with guilt.

The continuing bad weather and Bea's supposed convalescence kept them secluded for two days. The newspapers ran out of new details and rehashed the old ones. All the things Bea had considered herself. The only new comment in the scandal columns was that some people were playing least in sight. But she could not hide forever. The world had to be faced.

Meanwhile Simon had been to see Jones and Son to set them sniffing out the original source of the gossip. They were not hopeful but were willing to do their best.

On the third day a weak sun broke through the clouds and Jane took Bea, in an open carriage, to the park for the fashionable promenade. They were watched. Many of the people who had attended the wedding nodded but did not stop to talk. Only a few notorious gossips and one elderly man cut them dead. Bea tried not to mind but was heartened when Lady Leith stopped her carriage and exchanged a few words and Lord Truro asked loudly how they had been served at his estate. One of Jane's friends, Mrs Cowley, was walking with her married daughter and stopped to ask Bea if she was over her illness. Bea smiled softly and said, 'My husband over-reacted and rushed me back to town to see a doctor but I was over it in a few days.'

Mrs Cowley nodded. 'Then you will still be coming to the theatre this evening?' Bea lied and said she was looking forward to it and the carriage moved on.

Society was a fickle beast. It thrived on scandal but was scared of being implicated. Opinions swayed but few individuals wanted to openly join what might turn out to be the wrong side.

Simon had returned to his office at Whitehall as he had meetings scheduled concerning the up-coming Reform Bill. In the lobby he was hailed by Lord Derby, the prime minister. Several men stopped their own conversations to watch the meeting and heard Lord Derby say, 'A word with you Ridgeworth.' Simon slowed his pace as they walked slowly along the corridor as Derby was seventy and not in the best of health. Derby had been a life-long friend of Simon's father and done much to promote Simon's early career.

In the privacy of Simon's office, Derby sank into a chair and asked, 'What are we going to do about this mess?'

Simon breathed a sigh of relief. He had feared being dismissed as the scandal might reflect badly on the Reform Bill which was close to Derby's heart.

'I don't know, sir. Beatrice was the innocent victim of deceit.'

Derby nodded. His own long political career had not been free of scandal. His egalitarian views did not always meet with approval but he had worked doggedly for over twenty year's championing the rights of lesser individuals.

'You need to be bold,' the older man advised. 'The grand wedding was a good start, Entertain. Show the world you are unconcerned. Get your wife presented.'

It was sound advice but Simon did not know how to implement it.

Derby heaved himself to his feet and Simon accompanied him to the door. They shook hands and Derby said, 'Think about what I have said but do something soon.'

Simon had a lot to think about. Bea was already distressed that none of the invitations casually promised at the wedding reception had been forthcoming. On the other hand, none of the pre-accepted invitations had been cancelled.

Entertaining would be relatively easy. Enough of his friends and their wives had attended the wedding to make up a small party. Getting Bea presented was another matter. With the Queen still firmly entrenched in mourning some of her social duties had been taken over by the young Prince and Princess of Wales. Simon did not have reliable contacts in that circle. Bea needed a sponsor. His mother was out of the question and Jane, although respected, was socially insignificant.

He did not regret marrying Bea. He loved her and had promised to protect her. Her offer to live quietly as did his brother James' wife, tore at his heart. He ran a distracted hand through his hair and then covered his face. Men were not allowed to cry.

Why now? He kept asking himself. Fleming had died more than a year ago and Bea had built a new life for herself. Had he been selfish in taking Bea from her safe hiding place? She had dreaded being recognised. Who? Who of those knew the details could have let something slip? It was so unfair. They had been so happy for so few days. Once and for always had become a mantra. He would resign to save the precious Reform Bill if necessary but he would never give Bea up to satisfy the gossips.

Simon reluctantly gave his attention to the pile of documents on his desk.

Their visit to the theatre that evening was not quite the ordeal Bea had expected. Bea loved the theatre. She had attended several of Shakespeare's plays when they were performed in Cambridge. They were the only public events her father had ever taken her to. But she had never seen a comedy and was so caught up in the action on stage that she forgot about anyone watching her and just enjoyed herself.

The interval was trying as people roamed about, visiting other boxes or conversing in the foyer. Jane and Mrs Cowley swept Bea off to the ladies' room and kept up a lively conversation interspersed with nods and smiles to those they passed. Bea's jaw ached from the effort of keeping her chin up and a smile glued to her lips. Michael was also at the theatre but seated with some of his friends in the stalls. They all trooped up to the box and spoke with Simon and Mr Cowley while the ladies were away. Otherwise they were left alone.

At the end of the evening Bea thanked Mrs Cowley. The kind lady opened her eyes wide and laughed. 'It can be daunting getting back into company so soon after your marriage.' She gave a small chuckle, 'You imagine everyone is wondering what you got up to!'

Bea did not know if Mrs Cowley was just acting out of friendship for Jane or if she really believed the gossip did not refer to Bea. Either way it was greatly appreciated.

The next morning the worst of the gossip rags mentioned a certain lady??? flaunting herself in public. The pettiness annoyed Bea. She had been for a sedate carriage ride with a relation and a visit to the theatre with friends. On neither occasion had she done anything to draw attention. Far from cowing her the snide remarks stiffened her resolve to face the world with a calm smile even if she was a quivering jelly inside.

Their whole support team were carrying on as usual. When Michael had joined his friends last evening and was asked about the gossip, He had just looked blank and said, 'What gossip?'

Violet was more vocal. 'Do you think my mother would have a woman like that in our house!' Violet had exclaimed indignantly when probed for information. It carried weight because last year Violet had not been pleased to welcome a new cousin. Someone remembered Violet saying, 'She is so prim and proper she insists on wearing black for a husband she is glad to be rid of.' That did not sound like the behaviour of a brazen sinner.

Several days passed without any new accusations in the papers and Bea started to relax a little. She bravely risked going out without Jane to shield her. Escorted by Dora and Freddie she ventured to the shops and purchased an eye-catching hat. An unlikely choice for someone who planned to hide away, and wore that same afternoon.

Jane had persuaded Violet and her nearly-fiancé, Lord Ponsonby, to take Bea to an open-air concert held at the Royal Hospital in Chelsea. It was less formal than an evening event allowing people to circulate. 'A half-way house', was how Jane described it. Violet and Bea would never be fondest friends but a show of family unity was a good thing all round. Violet's young set was more open than their elders' and took Bea at face value. Bea had a sneaking suspicion that she was seen as Violet's chaperone rather than being under Violet's wing. But it helped to allay people's doubt. No mother would put her daughter in the care of a fallen woman.

More heartening than anything else for Bea was Simon's return to her bed. She had missed him while she was unwell and wondered if this was another high society convention. Her parents had slept together every night, no matter what the time of the month. Simon was as eager as before and taught her some new moves that delighted them both. Only in the day-time did she catch sight of his worried expression.

Chapter 24

Bea had abandoned having her breakfast in bed in favour of joining Simon. It gave them a chance to go through the papers together. The absence of any further innuendoes was welcome and Simon suggested they give a small dinner party. Bea was horrified. 'Will anyone come?' A refused invitation seemed even worse than not being invited elsewhere.

'We have support,' Simon assured her, 'but we have to be seen to stand on our own feet.'

It made sense but Bea waited anxiously for the invitations to be acknowledged. Another worry was that she had never given a party of any kind. Simon could help with the guest list but she had no idea how to be a hostess.

On Jane's advice Bea called a meeting of her senior staff. In the short time they had been serving her everyone, from Harris, the butler to the maid who assisted Dora, had taken Lady Ridgeworth to their hearts. Her natural good manners and her devotion to Lord Ridgeworth outweighed any scurrilous gossip. They had been with his lordship throughout the trials of his first marriage. Lady Monica's behaviour had of necessity been tolerated on the surface but they were not taken in by the charm she only used when she had an audience. Servants did not count and they had appreciated the new Lady Ridgeworth's courtesy in thanking them for their service.

To Bea's surprise the staff threw themselves into the venture. The chef suggested menus, pleased to find her ladyship did not need the French terms interpreted. His talents had been under-utilised of late and he looked forward to making her party memorable for its elegant cuisine.

Mrs Watts, the housekeeper liked having a mistress who respected her experience although she never took advantage. Before making any decision she always consulted her mistress and appreciated that she was thanked for her advice. Mrs Watts found a book on etiquette which they went through together. It did not seem quite so daunting after all. A hostess welcomed her guests according to their rank, seated them accordingly and made sure known rivals were kept apart. She also had to make sure everyone had a chance to join in the conversation.

'What do they talk about? Bea asked. Mrs Watts pursed her lips, more to hide a smile than in censure. 'Well, my lady, as you know, servants are deaf, dumb and blind unless told to do something.'

'What nonsense! I am not asking you to divulge secrets!' Bea laughed.

'In that case I suggest you ask what interests them and just listen. If anyone seems left out, you ask their opinion so they can join it.'

Bea thought it sounded very like running a bookshop.

All the invited guests accepted. They were mostly from Simon's political circle and would bring their wives. Jane would be there too, escorted by Michael. Bea invited Lady Leith and a friend to keep the numbers even. All seemed to be going well until Lady Leith wrote back to ask if she might bring her god-daughter, Lady Marchant.

Bea and Simon were at the breakfast table and he looked up when Bea gave a worried exclamation. 'I can't refuse but we will be short of two men.'

'I'll get Peters, my secretary, to fill in and I know plenty of single men who are willing to came at short notice if it means a free meal. Will that do?'

Bea did not care if he invited the coalman and Simon laughed as she said it. 'Peters will be quite acceptable. And Lady Marchant will be a valuable asset. She is one of Princess Alexandra's ladies.'

On the day of the dinner Bea was wracked with nerves. What if she did something wrong? This was one occasion when neither Jane nor Simon could be constantly by her side. She had dressed with care in a gown of dark rose silk that added some colour to her cheeks and wore the diamond necklace and earrings Simon had given her earlier.

'Good luck,' Dora said as Bea went down to join Simon in the hall ready to greet their guests as they arrived.

Lady Leith came first and introduced Lady Clara Marchant, Countess of Shortwood. She was a little older than Bea and bore a marked resemblance to the Princess of Wales. Simon bowed and the ladies curtsied. They exchanged conventional greetings, spoken by Lady Marchant in a slight foreign accent. It was all very polite but Bea felt she was being thoroughly assessed.

The other guests followed shortly after. They were all older than Bea, except Michael who looked around with a grimace. 'You owe me a favour for this,' he whispered. 'Not my sort of thing at all.'

'Then it is doubly kind of you to come and support me.'

Jane had arranged to give Bea a secret sign when it was time to change the courses and, later to take the ladies into the drawing room.

Bea led the way to the dining room on the arm of a gruff, elderly man whose name she had already forgotten. He patted her hand where it lay on his arm and muttered, 'Ease up, girlie. We don't bite.' Bea laughed as she caught the twinkle in his eyes. 'Thank you,' she whispered back.

The dinner party was a quiet and dignified success. Bea enjoyed listening to and sometimes joining in the conversations. She read the newspapers and kept abreast of current affairs so it was not too difficult. Much of it was to do with Canada and the celebrations planned in honour of it becoming a Dominion. By contrast, when Bea led the ladies to the drawing room the talk turned to families, fashion and entertainments. Bea preferred the former.

As they took their leave Lady Leith handed Bea an envelope. 'An invitation to a soiree I am holding in celebration of Canada becoming a Dominion. The Prince and Princess of Wales will be the guests of honour.'

Bea was speechless. Lady Marchant nodded. 'The Princess is eager to meet you,' she said and moved away to say goodbye to some of the other guests.

'I don't know how to thank you,' Bea said, taking Lady Leith's hand.

Lady Leith gave and almost mischievous grin. 'Then you will not mind if I poach your footman. He has potential but will never gain respect if he is seen as your favourite.'

Bea was not sure what Freddie would have to say about that but remembering how he was enjoying his new status felt he would welcome a chance to prove himself.

When everyone else had left, Jane swooped in and whirled Bea around in a circle. 'You have passed the test! I did not dare to tell you beforehand in case it made you nervous.'

'I was nervous,' Bea replied. 'Thank you for being such a support.'

Later, when they were at last alone, Bea asked Simon, 'Did you know about this?' placing the precious invitation on her dressing table.

'Lady Leith asked me to visit her. She is the daughter of an earl and widow of a marquis and still holds a position of respect and influence in Society. Lady Marchant was deputising for the Princess of Wales before you were officially received.'

'Oh, how can I thank them?'

Simon grinned, 'You can thank me instead.'

Next morning Simon received a bulky envelope bearing Mr Jones heavy writing.

Simon drew Bea close. Whatever Jones had found, Bea had the right to know.

They read the letter first.

My Lord Ridgeworth.

You will find enclosed my report and supporting evidence. Does your lordship wish to take further action? I would suggest leaking this to the press but await your instructions.

Jones had excelled himself. His previous investigation of Fleming had ceased when the bogus marriage came to light but that gave him a head start. He had gone straight to Edinburgh and found that the Robinson Flemings were not generally well thought of. A previous Robinson Fleming had cleared his large land holdings of residents in order to run sheep. He had cast off his heir (Robert Robinson Fleming) in favour of a nephew, Arthur. RRF had continued to be a thorn in his father's side by setting up as a successful businessman but only using his last name. The nephew was a gambler and had been involved in a recent court case for assault. (see newspaper cutting).

Simon thumbed through the enclosures he found it.

The cutting reported a case heard at Cheltenham Magistrates Court on 19th March 1867.

Mr Arthur Robinson Fleming had assaulted Mr Williams at the St Patrick's Day race meeting. An argument had arisen over a case of mistaken identity. The combatants had continued to throw insults at each other in court and were both fined for disturbing the peace. (Refer to statements).

Most of the statements were only hearsay but it boiled down to the fact that Williams had mistaken ARF for his cousin, a financier who was married to a bookseller/bookkeeper? in Cambridge, Williams home town. Both men had been drinking and the argument was overheard by many people.

Mr Arthur RF had loudly condemned his cousin as a bad lot. He threw doubt on his parentage, his business dealings and called him a womaniser. It is interesting to note that Mr Robert RF did not live with his wife who moved to Italy last year for health reasons. He openly lived with a woman separated from her husband but was reputed have had other liaisons. I cannot say how the news spread but both the argument, assault and court case were conducted in the presence of many, unidentified listeners who may or may not have had contacts in London.

Bea sagged against Simon's shoulder. 'I am glad it was not one of our trusted friends.'

'I know you were fond of Rob,' Simon almost choked on the name, 'but letting this out will gain you sympathy and clear your name.'

'And blacken his,' Bea said sadly. Bea thought of all the good people who had gone out of their way to help her at a risk to their own reputations. 'Do what you think best. Nothing can hurt him now.'

Simon kissed her brow. 'You are too kind, Bea. Personally, I think it a just punishment.'

Epilogue

Ridgeworth Court. 24th December 1869

Simon paced the corridors of his ancestral home in Berkshire. Bea had been in labour since the early hours of the morning and it was now nearing midnight. And Simon was worried sick. Why was it taking so long? He had sent word to the London doctor who had been monitoring Bea but there was little chance of him getting here any time soon. The local doctor was in bed with influenza so Bea was left in the hands of a midwife, Jane and Dora.

Another cry from the bedroom tore at Simon's heart and he wanted to rush to her side again. He had stayed with Bea until the midwife told him he was doing more harm than good with his worrying and thrust him bodily from the room. Her parting words, 'She's a bit old to be having a first baby and doesn't need you crying on her shoulder,' did not inspire confidence.

Simon had been wearing the carpet thin ever since as he walked up and down, never more than a few yards from the bedroom door.

Dear God, please don't take her away from me, Simon prayed. He was not overly religious but who else could comfort him now?

Truro was downstairs drinking the best brandy. Noakes was as anxious as a dog guarding a bone and the entire staff were on edge. Even the dog, Scamp kept escaping from the kitchen to press his nose against the bedroom door.

Thank goodness for Jane's calm competence. She and Lily had come to spend Christmas and stay until after the birth which was not expected until mid-January. Jane had kept the household on an even keel since Bea failed to come downstairs for breakfast which was just as well. With Alan and his children also here for the holiday and more guests expected tomorrow the staff needed someone in authority to look to for the endless details Simon could not have cared less about.

All he cared about was suffering beyond his reach. Suffering brought about by his own unrestrained passion. Another cry made Simon reach for the door handle ready to rush to Bea's side when a trio of children appeared at the end of the passage.

Simon was jerked out of his own worry. This was no place for children. He had expected them to be fast asleep by now.

'Lionel and Sarah woke me up to ask if it is Christmas yet,' Lily explained. 'Then I strange noises and came to see what was happening.' Bea had become almost like a sister to lily and aunt to Lionel and Sarah. They all adored her and had been affected by the general unrest in the house. Lily was old enough to understand and was enjoying being the eldest for a change but Alan's children were still at the babies being delivered by a stork stage.

Lily came close to Simon and whispered, 'Lionel thinks Bea is going to die because a stork came and took her baby away. Just like his mama did.'

Simon did not know who had told the boy such a stupid tale but it was not his problem. He had more than enough to worry about. He turned Lily about and propelled her back to the youngsters. 'Their papa is in the library. Take them down to him.' Once they were safely out of sight, Simon returned to his position by the bedroom door.

Everything had gone ominously quiet. Was that worse than Bea's screams?

Simon had never known any torment like this. The scandal had been harrowing at the time but soon forgotten. The scandal sheets had lapped up the new information and transformed Bea into an innocent girl taken advantage of by a trusted family friend. Now Bea was accepted everywhere and was well on her way to being a renowned political hostess. She had so much to live for.

For him. She had promised once and for always. Simon knew he was being irrational. Bea's torment was his fault. How could she possibly love him after this?

The bedroom door opened. Dora beamed and said, 'You have a son.'

Simon rushed past her into the bedroom and fell on his knees beside the bed. Bea was propped up on pillows and holding a white bundle. She smiled and held out her hand. Simon could hardly see her through his tears but she looked more beautiful than ever before. 'I love you, Bea. I thought I was going to lose you,' he croaked.

Bea shook her head. 'Once and for Always, remember. Once and for Always.'